FIREBIRD

Annabel Joseph

Scarlet Rose Press
Atlanta, Georgia

I would be remiss if I did not thank MalcolmD and Nemith for their help and inspiration in imagining the rope scene that takes place in Chapters Thirteen and Fourteen. Thanks also to Ibid for educating me on the ins and outs of the male orgasm, and the entire AIAMITLTGMBFO group on Fetlife.com for so generously feeding my fantasies.

I also need to thank my husband for his patience and support, and my trusty editors, Audrey and Venessa, for brutal honesty and helping me see what I'm too close to see.

And lastly, a belated thank-you to Low, who lives where laughter meets kink. Thanks for tickling my imagination time and time again.

CHAPTER ONE

Prosper stood in the wings in her wispy white tutu, a sparkling tiara in her upswept orange locks. Her face itched, but she didn't dare scratch it. She couldn't chance ruining her makeup, although the heavy foundation made her want to rake her nails across her face. Beside her, nine identical girls in white tutus waited and fidgeted, going up and down on their toes. She scuffed her shoes across the floor, then looked over at the ten dancers waiting on the other side of the stage. She glanced up into the light rigging and blinded herself.

Damn it. All to avoid looking at him. Jackson Spencer, the new choreographer. Tall, fine, blond haired and blue eyed, and stronger and sexier than any man had a right to be. She'd already caught his eyes twice trying to steal peeks at him. What was he doing, standing there against the back wall?

Watching. It felt like he was always watching her.

She knew she was just being paranoid. She supposed he came to watch the performances, to study the dancers' strengths. She'd seen him wandering around backstage several times last week. Once she'd even run into him on her way out of the dressing room. It had felt like hitting a wall. He'd mumbled "excuse me" and righted her. She'd chanced one look into his blue eyes and been burned by their intensity. Why did he always have that intent look in his eyes?

He was an artist, that's why. He didn't mess around. The dancers could sense that already. He was going to choreograph a new *Firebird*; everyone was talking about it. Kristen and Blake, the lead principals, were already looking back at older productions for ideas on characterization. Prosper thought if she was lucky, she might be cast as one of the twelve princesses, but she almost thought she'd be better back in the ranks of Kostchei's minions. Safer. If Jackson Spencer turned those intense eyes on her in rehearsal, if he wasn't pleased with her work, ugh. She would die.

Prosper squeezed her eyes shut. Her crazy perfectionist issues. She had bigger, more important things to think about. Glenna, her roommate, had told her earlier in the week that her cousin was coming to New York to move in. Which meant Prosper would have to move out. She'd made a few calls about apartments and realized she'd never in a million years be able to afford one unless she got a job. Well, a second job. Corps dancers didn't make very much money. She'd need a job she could do around the never-ending schedule of rehearsals, classes, and shows. She already knew she'd end up waitressing again. Waitressing or bartending was pretty much the most convenient, quick way for dancers to supplement the pittance they made in the corps.

Prosper sighed and dug one toe into the floor. Her pointe shoes were a mess. She'd be called on the carpet by Lawrence, the director, if he noticed. She needed to get her act together and find an affordable place to call home and a second job. And to accomplish all that, she needed to stop daydreaming about scruffy blond hair and amazing blue eyes.

Just one more glance. She'd look back at him once more before her entrance. She stole a peek from beneath her heavily made-up lids. He stood with his back against the wall, his arms crossed over his chest. She took in the blue jeans that accentuated the definition of his thigh muscles. Her gaze lingered on the distinct bulge at the top of his legs, then traveled up the long torso to the broad shoulders, then up to his eyes—

Staring right at her. Caught. Kayla tugged at her elbow, and Prosper realized she'd almost missed her cue.

That night she stayed up late imagining him lecturing her for not paying attention, right before he rolled up his sleeves and pulled her over his lap.

Jackson watched as the dancers trickled into the studio for daily class, shedding their sweaters and jackets to reveal their trim, muscular bodies. They all moved with that smooth grace dancers possessed that resulted from being utterly at home in your well-trained torso and limbs. He thought he probably walked the same, although he rarely danced anymore. He'd left that behind the year he'd turned twenty-six, and now, almost ten years later, he didn't miss it one bit, preferring choreography to dance hands down.

He'd just begun his stint as a guest choreographer at the Townsend Ballet last week. He'd had plenty of work back home in Chicago, but he was excited about dipping his toes into the New York dance scene, if only for a while. Right now it was late October—*Nutcracker* season—but rehearsals for the spring season were about to begin. He was contracted to stage a new version of Stravinsky's *Firebird* to celebrate the centennial of the ballet, and he was meeting with the company director today to discuss casting.

The dancers knew why he was there. He felt the nerves in the room. He didn't smile. He wasn't here to be friendly, to play bitch boy to the overweening egos of the principals, or to coddle the corps with simple, mincing steps. He was here to create something beautiful and affecting, and that would only come with a lot of hard work and bruised egos. And the talents of a certain dancer named Prosper Ware.

He had decided on her for the lead role the first time he'd seen her dance. Her technique was so beautiful, her body so slender and perfectly proportioned. He intended to cast Prosper as his Firebird, and Blake, the tallest principal male, as Prince Ivan. Choose one of the primas to play the Tsarina. He could already imagine Prosper picking through the steps with that precise manner she had. And her petite size—it was perfect. Now he just had to convince Lawrence to take a chance on an unproven dancer from the corps.

He shifted when he saw her enter and move to her place at the barre. God, that flaming orange hair. Even her warm-up stretches possessed a quality of movement that set her above the crowd. He was still staring when the ballet master clapped his hands to call the company to order. Lawrence entered soon afterward. He greeted Jackson as he came to stand beside him against the wall. The gossiping quieted, and the dancers lined up by rank to begin the exercises. Principals, soloists, corps, all in their places. As class commenced, Lawrence pointed to Kristen, the lead principal female.

"Kristen is very dependable and highly talented. I'm assuming you want her for the Firebird."

"Mm. Maybe the Tsarina."

Lawrence looked surprised but deferred to him with a nod. "Elsa, then. Although she's not as quick as Kristen."

Jackson pointed to Prosper. "That one's really quick. The redhead."

"Mm. Prosper Ware."

"I was thinking about her for the Firebird."

Lawrence chuckled. "Yes, her hair is quite fiery, isn't it?" He sobered when he noticed Jackson wasn't laughing. "You're serious?"

"I think she'd be perfect. Her size, her quickness."

"She's only a corps dancer." Lawrence's voice rose over the plingpling of the piano, but he dropped it as a few dancers glanced their way. "Just because she's got red hair—"

"This has absolutely nothing to do with her hair. Her movement is perfect, as careful as I've ever seen in a dancer—corps or principal or anything in between. Why is she buried in the back of your company?"

"Because she's not a show person, Jackson. Yes, she has flawless technique, but she won't be able to do it. Trust me."

"How can you be so sure?"

The two men faced off, arms crossed over chests. Jackson would stand his ground. He knew from experience that matters of casting could make or break a ballet. Of course after many years of managing ballet companies, Lawrence knew it too. With a harried sigh, the older man guided Jackson into the hall.

"Look, I understand you don't want to hear this, but I know my dancers. She doesn't have the experience—"

"That's bullshit and you know it."

"I'd love to see you choreograph a new *Firebird* on one of our prima ballerinas, but Prosper—no, I don't see it."

"I do see it. She can do it."

"It will cause a revolt! You can't just go plucking unknowns from the corps and choreographing productions on them."

"There are plenty of other roles for your principals."

Lawrence frowned, but Jackson sensed victory. The director had worked too hard to lure Jackson to the Townsend to risk alienating him right at the start.

"Fine. If you'd like to try Prosper in the role, you're welcome to. But I'm afraid you'll find the most exciting thing about her is that shock of orange hair."

Jackson pursed his lips, biting back any further retorts so as not to press his luck. The men returned to the class to discuss the casting of the other roles, but Jackson's gaze kept returning to her. At one point he caught her looking back at him with her deep green eyes. She quickly dropped her gaze. But he continued to stare, enthralled by the precision of her pointe work, the fluidity of her *port de bras*. The perfect arch of her foot.

Now that he had his Firebird, he couldn't wait to get started. There was something so compelling about the story of the magical bird that was both a blessing and a curse to the prince who captured her. The choreographers of a century ago had made it too tame, too innocent. He thought the darker themes of the story needed to be brought to the fore. He saw the whole sexy, violent story coming to life in his imagination. The immortal Kostchei with his macabre band of followers; the twelve abducted maidens, vulnerable and pure; the Tsarina and Prince Ivan, star-crossed lovers trapped by a madman; and the skittish Firebird pulling out her red feather and putting everything back to rights.

Icy wind blew up the narrow city street and sliced through the wool coat and sweater Prosper wore. She shivered and hugged herself. It was midmorning, but she still felt sleepy and slow. She'd been up late the night before thinking about Jackson Spencer again. She really needed to pull herself together. He would figure out how she felt about him if she didn't get herself under control. He would feel the lust coming off her in waves, lust aimed right at him. What were they called, those chemicals? Pheromones? She must be dripping with them. She must be silly with wild, undisciplined pheromones by now.

Why was she so hot for him? She'd never had much of a sex drive, not like the drive she'd felt lately. She'd read in his bio that he'd danced in a Chicago company years ago. She felt jealous of the lucky ballerinas he must have partnered. How had they managed to dance with him so near? With him touching them? She would fall right off pointe and probably break her leg if he put his hands on her. He must have been spectacular at partnering. He was so masculine and sexy. His eyes missed nothing, and his body was so solid, so strong.

Ugh, enough. She ducked into a small coffee shop and forced herself to think about something besides Jackson. She scanned the specials, but nothing caught her eye.

"Just the usual, Derick." She smiled at the middle-aged man behind the counter.

"One mocha cappuccino coming right up." His voice sounded loud in the nearly empty space. "Have a seat. We're not busy. I'll bring it out to you."

She nodded as he turned to make the drink. She scanned the display of free reading materials beside the counter and picked up the local underground mag to see if any of the bars were hiring. There were several pages of ads in the back, and she leafed through them looking for the job classifieds. She was flipping past the personals when a header caught her eye. A small caricature of a cat dressed like a dominatrix, cracking a whip. A tagline beside it. *Fetish.*

"Order up," Derick sang out, sweeping over to deliver her drink. She quickly pushed the mag to the side. Since the shop was empty, he crowded into the booth beside her to chitchat, although what she really wanted was to gawk at the fetish ads. After fifteen minutes she'd finished her coffee and said good-bye, shoving the paper in her dance bag. The moment she stepped back on the street, the warm coffee inside her froze.

She walked faster on her way to the theater. Time for class. She'd have to look over the kinky ads later. Just for fun, she told herself. No way would she answer one. She wouldn't place an ad either, although she found herself crafting one in her mind. *SWF, 25, shy, petite, red hair. ISO someone to control her, to tell her what to do. To spank her, to torment her, to fuck her. Scruffy blond hair and unbelievably intense eyes a plus.* Oh, probably too many words. It would take way too many words to explain what she wanted, what she needed. But it would be fun to read the other ads and see what other kinky New Yorkers were in search of.

Prosper ducked into the building. She was going to be late if she didn't hurry. Again the image of Jackson rolling up his sleeves came to mind. *Enough, Prosper.* That's all she needed was to go into class and be confronted with him, larger-than-life, with that image rolling around in her head. And he would be there. He always was, at least for a while, looking around as they cycled through the same boring exercises. She wondered if he'd made his decisions about casting yet.

She scurried to her place just as the ballet master called them to attention. She did some quick stretches and turned the wrong way to begin. Damn. Jackson stood not ten paces away, wearing his usual serious expression, along with a loose white T-shirt and baggy sweats. Only he could make gym pants sexy.

She disciplined her mind to the exercises, to executing each movement perfectly. She became so involved in her work that she was shocked to look up and find him standing beside her. She blushed, knowing it would show in her pale cheeks. She flitted a look at his face. His gaze was fastened to her feet.

He spoke then, so low she was certain the dancers to the right and left couldn't hear.

"Prosper, I'd like to speak to you after class."

She nodded, not looking at him. What could he want with her? It wasn't his job to critique or reprimand the dancers, not that Prosper thought she was doing anything wrong. But if he didn't want to comment on her technique, then why did he need to talk to her?

After class he waited for her by the door. The other dancers watched as she left and followed him down the hall. She was more aware than ever of his imposing size and musculature as he led her into Lawrence's office and through to the small conference room. He smelled fresh, like deodorant or aftershave. She trailed behind, staring at the light freckles on the back of his neck, his golden hair. He ushered her in and shut the door behind her. He didn't sit down, and neither did she. Instead he faced her, his arms crossed over his chest.

"You look anxious," he began. "Don't be. You're not getting called on the carpet for anything you've done wrong. In fact, I've been observing class and come to the conclusion that you're one of the most talented dancers here."

Oh my God. "Thanks, Mr. Spencer. I try."

"I have a role for you, Prosper. A career-starting one. As you know, I'm here to stage Stravinsky's *Firebird*, and I'd like you to dance the lead."

"The lead? The Firebird?" She tried to exude a calm, self-assured demeanor at this news. But the Firebird, the title role! She was both ecstatic and terrified. "I... God... Wow. I would love to. But Lawrence might not—I'm not one of the principals—"

"I spoke to Lawrence. It took some convincing, but he's agreed I can give you a try. I think you have the talent and the ability." He studied her, pulling at his lip. "But I'm not yet convinced you have the drive."

"Oh, I do, I swear. I do. I want to do it. I'm just a little—"

"Surprised?"

"To put it lightly. Yes."

"I hope you realize, Prosper—" He stopped. "Prosper. I've never heard that name before. Is there a story behind it?"

"It's short for Prosperity."

"Prosperity!" He seemed to like that, repeating it. "Prosperity Ware. Fantastic name."

"Thank you." She was spellbound by the warmth of his rare smile.

"Well, Prosperity, if you accept this role..." His smile faded, replaced by familiar stern lines. "If you accept this role, I'm going to expect perfection from you. I've wanted to stage *Firebird* for some time. I have some progressive ideas for it. This won't be Fokine's cutesy ballet."

He let that sink in, fixing her with a look that reminded her to a frightening degree of the way he looked at her in her dreams.

"I'm going to expect diligence, stamina, courage, patience," he continued. "Everything a prima ballerina needs to have, particularly one who's having a ballet choreographed on her."

"Yes, Mr. Spencer. I understand. Absolutely."

"You're sure you have what it takes?"

"Yes." She imbued her voice with all the confidence she could muster. "I definitely do."

"We'll see. The part is yours conditionally. We'll do some work together and see how things progress. I'd like you to meet me in the small rehearsal room tomorrow after class."

"Okay. Yes. I'll be there. I'm so excited to work with you!" *Tone it down, Prosper. Don't simper.*

He nodded and led her to the door. "I'm excited too. I'll see you tomorrow. Come ready to work hard."

And with that she was dismissed. His calm, detached manner did nothing to dampen her joy. She ran to the costume closet and collapsed on the floor in a heap, muffling her squeals in a pile of tutus.

She wished she could scream the news from the rafters, but he had only given the part to her conditionally. But she would show him. She would show all of them that she was talented, that hard work paid off. She rested her cheek against the scratchy tulle, her heart racing with excitement. Not only was she going to dance the role of the Firebird, but she was going to be working with Jackson Spencer every day. It might take weeks for him to block the steps with her and the other dancers, weeks of working side by side with him. Then serious rehearsals after the new year.

The ballet was scheduled to headline the spring season in February. That was a solid three months of collaboration. She just hoped her horny fantasies wouldn't interfere with her ability to work with him. She hugged herself. She knew she could do it. She would help Jackson realize his vision and mount an unforgettable ballet. She floated through the rest of the day dreaming of birds and princes, danger and bravery, and Jackson's unforgiving stare.

CHAPTER TWO

Jackson could see the orange hair in his peripheral vision the moment she arrived for rehearsals. "Come in," he said. "Close the door." He shut the curtain to the window beside him with a snap of his wrist but left the other curtain open. "I've been waiting. Class ran over?"

"No." She dropped her dance bag and crossed to the barre. "Some people wanted to know what I was doing here with you."

He realized his hands were clenched at his sides. *Settle down, Jack.* He'd been waiting too long to begin work with her. He was antsy. He watched her stretch for a moment, then looked away as his groin begin to tighten. Her lines destroyed him.

"What did you tell them?" he asked to distract himself. "All your curious friends. Did you tell them you were dancing the Firebird?"

"You said conditionally, so I haven't said anything yet." She finished stretching and turned to him, standing still. Waiting. Even the way she waited was alluring. He needed to get her moving, get her on her toes instead of this excruciating stall.

"Come on. Center."

She moved to the middle of the room. It was called the small rehearsal room, but it wasn't small, only not as large as the larger rehearsal hall where the company took class and where entire ballets were rehearsed in front of the mirror. This room was only mirrored on one side. He turned her toward it.

"So you know the basic story of *Firebird*?"

"Yes, pretty much. The prince finds her in a garden, dances with her—"

"Captures her."

Prosper fell silent.

"He captures her and refuses to release her unless she agrees to return when he asks."

"Yes." She nodded. "A very practical monarch."

"Yes, practical, but also selfish. And driven to subdue a creature both weaker and more powerful than himself."

He watched as a blush crept across the back of her neck. My God, she was so close he could smell her, fresh soap and faint perfume.

"But you're not dancing the prince," he said, collecting himself. "And really, his story doesn't concern you. After you tell him the secret of how to defeat Kostchei and rescue his princess, you fly away, and he's left with his safe, proper wife."

"Mmm."

"But I think he remembers the Firebird his whole life. Do you know why?"

She turned her head, the blush spreading across her cheeks. "Why?"

"Because she was the only creature of her kind he'd ever seen in his life."

She drew in a soft breath. He was going to lick her in a moment, all the way from her nape to her staid ballerina bun. *Focus. Show her what to do, instead of staring at her neck and imagining a collar there.*

"Can you do this with your arms?"

He showed her some of the birdlike movements he'd been thinking about. She did what he showed her, better and more gracefully than him. He took her through a few more steps, broadly at first, then precisely. "Are you still being a bird?" he reminded her from time to time. But she was, and it was a thrill to stand near her and watch her move through space, bringing his steps to life. He tried not to touch her too much, although he ached to. A few nudges, a few pats to isolate body parts to show how they should move. That was all he would allow himself. This was business. He had a ballet to create. He wasn't here spending time with her to get his rocks off. *Concentrate, idiot.*

"I'm still thinking," he said when they finally paused. "I'm just trying to see the best way to tell the story through the movements."

She nodded, standing at rest but still ready to move as soon as he guided her in some way. God, those eyes—they were so green. He wanted to ask where on earth she'd gotten those eyes, but instead he said, "They'll hate you, you know."

Her face tensed. She bit her lip, but she didn't ask who. She knew. Everyone.

Everyone would hate her for what he was doing. The principals would hate her for taking a role above her station. Her fellow corps dancers would ostracize her now that she'd been elevated from their ranks. And he would make her life hell for the next three months or so, mounting his new vision of an old classic on her slender back and quick feet.

"I don't have a lot of friends here anyway," she said.

"Why is that?"

She shrugged. "I'm not good at the game. Kissing up. Politics. I try to let my work speak for itself. I try to be as perfect as possible and let things fall where they may."

He studied her. He believed her. There was something about her, a focused intensity that compelled him. "Okay, good. Perfect is good. The part is yours. I'm going to announce it and do the rest of the casting. I'll have Blake dance Prince Ivan. He seems best suited. Have you danced with him before?"

She shook her head with an incredulous expression. Blake was the leading principal male. He supposed it was like telling the invisible girl in school she was going on a date with the prom king.

"Okay," he said, clapping his hands. "Back to center again."

"Oh my God!" Glenna and Katie squealed over the daily recap of her rehearsal with Jackson while they applied makeup for the evening's performance.

"How the hell do you dance with him breathing down your neck like that?" Katie asked.

Prosper rolled her eyes. "He doesn't breathe down my neck."

"We saw him," said Glenna. "He definitely does. And he was staring at your ass."

"For ages," Katie agreed. "Totally staring."

"He was not." It had only been a few days, but it was already starting to get old. Aside from Glenna and Katie, the other dancers snubbed her, and she had a feeling Glenna and Katie only talked to her to hear more about Jackson Spencer.

She understood the attraction, unfortunately. It was a constant battle to act natural around him, to not let her eyes linger on his bulging arms or his thick thighs or the glimpse of flat, defined stomach whenever he stretched his arms over his head. Of course his gruff personality threw frigid water on any hot fantasies she had, and she had plenty of them, an entire repertoire following on the heels of the sleeve-roll-and-spank dream.

Glenna was about to launch into another barrage of questions when Kristen and the other principals arrived in the room. Kristen planted herself at a mirror on the other side of Glenna and began rattling through her makeup case. Glenna turned her back on Kristen, a wonderful show of solidarity. But it offered Prosper little protection from Kristen's wrath. The prima glanced over at Prosper with a haughty look as she lined her lips, then smacked them together.

"Bitch."

Glenna gasped, but Prosper shook her head. "Ignore her," she said to Glenna. Prosper fussed over invisible flaws in her foundation, trying to follow her own advice, but Kristen seemed determined to be heard.

"Look. She thinks she's a star already. Too bad he'll probably recast in a week, once he realizes she can't do it."

"Don't be a cat," Blake said to Kristen, his usual dance partner. "Leave her alone."

Kristen applied her false eyelashes and copious eye shadow. She was dancing the lead in *The Nutcracker* and had most certainly assumed the Firebird part was hers. "You know, I didn't work my way up to principal to have the best parts stolen by a bitchy little upstart from the corps."

Her friend Elsa, another principal, giggled. "You're mean."

"I don't know what he sees in her," Kristen sniffed, appealing to Blake. "And you're the one who'll have to drag her around the stage trying to make her look good. No way she can pull this off on her own. I mean, the Firebird! That's a really challenging role!"

Blake slanted a skeptical look at Prosper through dark eyes, flipping back his black wavy hair. He was the epitome of tall, dark, and handsome. Chiseled features, olive skin. Being one of very few straight male dancers, he got a lot of attention, from the principal ballerinas down to the groupies in the corps. At one time, like all the other girls, she'd had a crush on him. She saw in the mirror what he thought of her and quickly dropped her gaze. He turned his back on her, focusing on Kristen.

"You get all the best roles, Kris. Let her have this one. You got the Tsarina—"

"I don't want the fucking Tsarina. The Tsarina doesn't even dance on pointe. Next thing he'll be casting us principals as fucking dancing princesses."

"Well, they do need twelve," Blake said, baiting her.

Elsa made a hissing sound and rolled her eyes.

"Don't listen to them," said Glenna under her breath. "Jealous bitches. That's all they are. Jealous and rude."

"I know." Prosper tried not to care, but there was an uneasy feeling in the pit of her stomach that wouldn't go away.

When she arrived for rehearsals the following day, Blake was stretching by the barre. She stopped inside the door, remembering how he'd looked at her in the dressing room the night before.

"Do you know him?"

She jumped. She hadn't heard Jackson come up behind her.

"No, I don't know him. Not really."

"Blake." Jackson beckoned him over. In her ear he said, "Lift your head up. Keep it up."

She tore her gaze from the floor as Jackson did the introductions.

"Blake, Prosper. Prosper, Blake."

Blake smiled at Prosper and shook her hand as if the evening before had never taken place. She forced her own smile in reaction. Jackson ushered them to the center of the floor.

"Prosper and I have already been rehearsing. I'd like to try out a few sequences I've been thinking about, to see if they work."

"Sure," said Blake. Jackson directed them through some partnering without music, just marking steps. He stood back and watched as they got a feel for one another.

"Shorter than you're used to, yeah?" he asked when Blake almost strangled her reaching for her neck instead of her waist.

Blake chuckled. "I'll get it."

"Here," Jackson said. "Like this."

Jackson took Prosper's hand and stood behind her, taking Blake's place. He was even taller than Blake, Prosper realized. It was a trick of proportion. His thicker body made it seem as if he should be shorter. They did the same sequence, but Blake's tentative partnering was gone, replaced by hands that propelled her.

All her daydreams about being partnered by him were forgotten. The reality was a hundred times better. Jackson turned her, steadied her as she reached back, took her hand as she went into an arabesque on pointe. She extended the lines, his fingers alone holding her perfectly balanced. His hands didn't waver, didn't move an inch as she threw him her body weight, her momentum. Their eyes met for one intense moment.

"You see?" he said to Blake. He released her, and she felt loose and heavy again.

Blake took over. His fingers and hands felt lackluster after Jackson's unyielding grip.

"No," said Jackson as they began the steps. "You're supposed to be trapping her. Hold her. Grasp her. You can't let her get away. Prince Ivan traps the Firebird against her will. And you—" He pointed to Prosper. "I need to see fear in your eyes. This sequence is going to be very dark and sexual. Attraction, capture, desire."

Prosper flushed hot at his words, but Blake shook his head.

"Desire? Attraction? She's a bird."

"She's not just a bird. It's not that simple. She's a wild, exotic, mysterious creature you're drawn to. Forget that she's a bird—think of her as an impulse. A fantasy. Plenty of years to settle down with your prim Tsarina. You have this one chance in the dark garden with the Firebird. It has to be good enough to convince her to return later and save your life. Yes?"

Prosper stood with her hands behind her back, staring off. Wild, exotic? Mysterious? She had been miscast. She read it in Blake's eyes as they swept over her, in the derisive tilt of his lip.

"Again," Jackson snapped.

Four times. Four times he ended up having to partner her to show that clod Blake what he had in mind. She picked up everything instantly, reproduced it easily, but Blake acted as if Jackson was asking him for the moon. Blake didn't like her, fine. That much was obvious. It was fucking churlish, though, to let it show. He figured one of the other two principal males could dance it better, but he really needed Blake's height.

Hopefully in time Blake and Prosper would gel together. As soon as he thought it, a part of him rebelled. He wanted her to remain the elusive, mysterious Firebird. It was Blake who would need to open up to her, figure out how to desire her, at least onstage.

He considered sticking around the theater to watch Prosper in the show that evening. But watching would be an empty thrill for him now that he'd partnered her. He remembered the feel of her small hand in his, and her waist under his fingers, slim and sinuous, the thin leotard the only thing between his fingertips and her warm, smooth skin. And her gaze when he'd propped her in the arabesque. Ah, she'd felt it too.

He sighed and headed home instead, paced around his apartment, and finally booted up his computer. A little cyberporn would take the edge off. But instead he Googled Prosper Ware, uncovering a few ballet-related pages. A small bio on the Townsend website outlined her dance schools and a few short stints in companies in Cincinnati and Dayton. He learned her birthday and that she was twenty-five years old. She looked younger. She was far too young for him at any rate. Why was he still thinking about it?

He clicked off-line and rubbed his eyes. Ten o'clock. Maybe he would go out. He leafed through the nightlife magazine he'd picked up at the diner, looking for a band to see or a likely nightclub to find the type of girl he sought, only to be sidetracked by the personals section.

Fetish. Seven pages full.

"One mocha cappuccino!"

Prosper closed the magazine as Derick swept to the table with her drink. It had been a week since she'd had time to pick up another mag, another week gone by that she hadn't found an after-hours job, and now she was wasting time looking at fetish ads.

"Whatcha reading?"

"Oh nothing. Just—"

"Personals, huh? Looking for love?"

Prosper laughed at his teasing. "I'm too busy, Derick."

"You're never too busy for love." He craned his head to look at the paper. "Any likely candidates?"

She shrugged. "I'll let you know if I find someone. But actually I was looking through these ads to find a job."

"A job? I thought you were a dancer."

"I am. But it's expensive to live in New York."

"Tell me about it, honey." Prosper knew Derick's real job was working at an art gallery, another job that didn't pay quite enough. To her relief a group of customers entered, drawing Derick back to the counter. Again she turned to the fetish ads.

Lots of male submissives, lots of professional dommes, a smattering of couples looking for a third. Not really what she wanted, even if she was looking. Which she wasn't. Some single men looking for a girl on the side, some swingers seeking couples or play partners, a few older doms looking for nubile young flesh to mark. She was about to close the paper when an ad at the bottom of the last page caught her eye.

SWM, mid 30s, dom, safe, sane, seeks fit, petite sub F 20-30ish
Must be sensual, crave training, accept pain.
Play partner only, no commitment. Pleasure guaranteed.
Red hair a plus. Let's meet & talk. George (A405)

She stared at the ad a long time. *Fit, petite. Red hair a plus.*
Pleasure guaranteed.

No way was she answering a personal ad. She wasn't that desperate, was she? She wasn't ready for the complexity of a relationship with a new dom.

But George (A405), this dom, wanted no commitment. *Play partner only.* And he apparently had a thing for red hair.

She bit her lip between sips of coffee, trying to talk herself out of doing something she really shouldn't do. He could be a predator or some married guy sneaking around getting his kink on. But what harm would there be in meeting and talking? With a sigh, she closed the mag and stuffed it in her bag. This was ridiculous. Truly, the idea was ridiculous. She needed to focus. She was dancing the lead in a ballet. She had to find a new place to live and a source of supplemental income. These were things she *needed* to do.

She did not *need* to enter into a new D/s relationship right now.

No.

After class she drifted to the rehearsal room and found Jackson as agitated as she was. It was just the two of them. Solo work again.

They exchanged brief greetings and got right to business. They'd been working daily together for almost two weeks now and still hadn't exchanged more than a few words, most on the first day.

But it didn't matter; they communicated perfectly. He explained what he wanted, and Prosper tried to deliver it. If she didn't get it, she tried again. If she still didn't produce what he wanted, he would put his hands on her and show her what to do. It both thrilled and devastated her when that happened. She hated doing things wrong. She hated frustrating him. She hated the tense impatience she sometimes felt in his hands when he put them on her.

Today she saw it in his face. He explained a difficult combination and asked her to do it. She got it on the second try, and then he wanted it faster. She tried to concentrate on his barrage of instructions.

"Faster, faster! Toe, toe, toe...quickly!"

"I'm trying."

She did it again and again. He still wasn't satisfied.

"Not fast enough! And look at your arms. Sloppy." He clapped his hands at her. "Concentrate. Again!" He beat out the tempo on the floor with his foot, then clapped it, louder and louder. Just as she almost had it, he slapped her ass.

No, he didn't slap her. It wasn't a slap. It was a blow. She fell off pointe and spun on him. God, had he just spanked her? She backed away, rubbing at the sting.

"I'm sorry," he said. "I was trying to speed you up." He frowned, the offending hand now idle at his side. "I didn't mean to do that. Did it hurt?"

She crossed her arms over her chest and glared at him. "The speed you want for that combination hurts."

"I know. I know I ask a lot of you. Maybe we should just call it a day."

Prosper nodded and turned away, and crossed to pick up her bag. She could still feel the stinging outline of his hand on her ass, a sting that was familiar and yet, coming from him, unexpected and strange. She looked back at him jotting notes in his notebook. "Is everything okay?"

He looked up. "Uh, yeah, Prosper. Everything's fine, I'm just distracted today. We'll pick up tomorrow."

He dismissed her by turning back to focus on his notes.

3 CHAPTER THREE

As soon as Prosper got home from the evening performance, she ran to the bathroom and looked back over her shoulder in the mirror. She pulled up one side of her panties to reveal a faint bruise. Wow. He took his choreography seriously. She didn't want to know what he'd do if she ever really slaughtered his steps. For all her feigned outrage, the slap he'd delivered to her ass had stoked a fire she didn't need stoked, at least not around him. She went to her room and changed into pajamas, then looked down again at the paper lying on her bed. She'd thrown it in the trash three times already, only to dig it out again and open it to George's ad.

Fit, petite. Red hair a plus.

Pleasure guaranteed.

She sighed and worried the dog-eared pages between her fingers. She should just go to bed. She had to get up in the morning for an interview at a nightclub down the street. Against her better judgment, she crept out to Glenna's computer anyway and clicked it on. The sudden glare of the screen lit the dark apartment and made Prosper wince. Before she lost her nerve, she logged onto the magazine's website and navigated to the personals. She set up an account, scolding herself the whole time for being an idiot. It was too risky. He could be a maniac.

Well, she wouldn't tell him anything about her, not even her real name. Then if he turned out to be a disgusting, icky guy, she could just walk away. When she was logged on as Julie (M467), she searched until she found George's ad, and clicked on it. She typed a short note to leave in his in-box.

George,
My name is Julie. Fit, red hair too. <grins>
I've never answered an ad before,
but your pitch sounds appealing.

She stopped writing, unwilling yet to tell any more about herself. She'd leave it open, just express a little interest. She hit Send and took a deep breath. She would see what he wrote back. If he even wrote back.

Jackson looked at the smiling woman sitting across from him as he signaled the waiter for the check. He hoped the parting wouldn't be too awkward, although he didn't really know a nonawkward way of telling someone you had no intention of seeing them again. The submissive he'd met through his personal ad had fudged a little on the "fit" descriptor. She'd fudged a little on the age too. She was in her midfifties, he guessed. She actually looked similar to some of his mom's friends back home, except that his mom's friends didn't call him Master and outline all the ways they'd provide service to him.

He suppressed a shudder. He just wanted to get out of this situation with minimum damage to her psyche—and his. He waved off her offer to split the check and threw down some bills, anxious to leave the restaurant before she asked for his number, or worse, volunteered to come back to his place.

"Can I get you a cab?" he asked, trying to infuse his voice with an unmistakable, but gentle, finality.

"I drove." She forced a false and cheerful smile. "It was certainly nice to chat with you."

He tried to summon up a true smile. It was the least he could do for her in the face of his total rejection. "I hope you find what you're looking for, Myra. I just think I'm not it."

She nodded. "I suppose. I hope you find what you're looking for too."

His mind flew to Prosper, to movement and shyness and mystery. "I hope so too." They shared a stiff hug. "I'll walk you to your car."

"No. I'd rather you didn't. Good-bye, George." She turned her back on him and walked away. After a moment he turned in the other direction toward his house, trying to shake off pangs of guilt. Why should he feel like the villain? She was the one who had answered his ad, purporting to be something she was not. She wasn't fit; she wasn't anywhere near the age range he'd specified. Her hair was salt-and-pepper, not red. She was too slavey, too spineless to interest him. Too desperate.

But then he was desperate too. Why else would he even be trying this? Did he really expect to meet a decent woman this way? What kind of woman would look for a partner in the personal ads? Then again, he was looking for a partner in the personal ads, and he was basically normal. Mostly normal, apart from all the kink stuff he liked to do. But it wasn't worth it, not if he was going to end up in situations like this, meeting with people who were completely wrong for him and then feeling guilty for blowing them off. He wasn't even going to be in New York for very long. Better to just delete the ad and rely on porn for the few months he'd be here. Porn and fantasies of Prosper. No one would live up to her anyway, so what was the point?

He bounded up the stoop and into his house, determined to delete his ad before he changed his mind. He logged on to the website and found another message in his box from someone named Julie. He moved the mouse, the pointer hovering over the Delete button, but then curiosity got the best of him, and he opened it.

George,
My name is Julie. Fit, red hair too. <grins>
I've never answered an ad before,
but your pitch sounds appealing.

He stared at the message. Short and abrupt, nothing like Myra's meandering essay. He tapped his finger on the mouse, considering. Yesterday he would have been thrilled about the possibilities, but now he was skeptical. Was she worth the risk of another awkward meeting? But she met his criteria—or claimed to—and obviously wanted to know more. *Fit, red hair too.* He thought of Prosper, of all the things he dreamed of doing to her. If he could find someone like her, perhaps it would ease the ache just enough to make it bearable. His resolve began to ebb, and he clicked the Reply button. He'd write back and see where things went, but he wouldn't harbor any false hopes this time.

> *Julie,*
>
> *Thanks for your note. Glad I appealed to you. <g>*
> *My pitch is what it is, no games. I'm looking for fun and*
> *enjoyment. Not to brag, but I'm told I know what I'm doing.*
> *I'm new to the area, rather busy, and need*
> *the occasional "unwind." Want to meet? Talk?*

He reread it. Light, nonthreatening. Some controlled boasting but not over the top. He pushed Send and dressed quickly. Time for rehearsal. He didn't know if he'd be able face Prosper after actually spanking her ass—*spanking her ass*—yesterday. The look on her face when she'd spun on him. Priceless. Any hopes he'd harbored that she might secretly be into D/s disappeared at the outrage on her face. Not that he'd been testing her. It had just happened. He would have to be careful not to cross any more lines of propriety with her, regardless of the fantasies in his mind.

He walked down the street cursing his overactive imagination. Even the crisp late-autumn air couldn't cool him off when he started thinking about her. Her, whoever her was. The serious, focused Prosper he worked with every day, or the more sensual Prosper who haunted his dreams every night. He'd lain in bed last night thinking about his favorite new scenario. Prosper, nude, in the rehearsal room. Him running her through steps and combinations with a riding crop dangling from his fingers. When she took a wrong step or turned the wrong way, which never happened in real life, he'd raise the crop and give her a sharp thwack on the underside of her ass. She would yelp and apologize. He would gesture for her to repeat it, unwavering.

Fuck. He rearranged his rising cock and walked faster. No, not a good dream for now, out on the street, a block away from the theater. He looked up and did a double take. There she was, coming in the other direction. He slowed his pace, trying to time it so they would arrive at the door at the same time. Near the door she noticed him, slowed, held back. Scared of another spanking?

"Hi, Prosper."

"Hello."

He opened the door for her. "You're late."

"I was getting breakfast at that coffee shop down the street. The waiter always talks my ear off."

"What coffee shop? There's one nearby?"

They both crossed the lobby to hang up their coats. A dozen other dancers milled around, but he only saw her.

"Yeah. It's called Coffee Place," she said. "Creative, huh?"

He was spellbound. Like a true fetishist, he noticed everything about her—the novelty of her light laughter, the graceful way she stretched to hang her coat.

"It's beside the dry cleaners. It's not fancy, and it's almost always empty, but the coffee is good."

"Oh well, that's the important thing, yes?"

That lovely laughter again. How had he never heard her laugh? Didn't they ever joke around during rehearsals? No, they didn't. He barely even smiled when he was working with her. Trying too hard, he supposed, to hide how he really felt. Trying too hard to resist spanking her tight little ass. If she still held that against him, she wasn't showing it now, thank goodness.

"Is Blake rehearsing with us today?" she asked.

"No. Just you and me."

He thought they could use Blake. A chaperone. The other dancers were watching them. *No one knows. No one knows the things you think about her.* Still, it made him uncomfortable, all those eyes on him. Someone would see. He took a deep breath and gestured to the rehearsal room.

"Well, it's time. After you."

She ducked her head in that way that drove him wild and went ahead of him. Still aware of the many pairs of eyes on them, he tried not to stare at her ass in her tight little sweats.

He stayed for the show that night, a glutton for punishment. He hoped Julie came through for him. Anything to take his mind off this girl. When he got home, he logged on to find a handful of messages but no Julie. The messages contained nothing worth responding to. Mostly offers for massages and one badly misspelled message asking if "bleech blond hair insted of red iz ok????" But just as he was about to log off, he got a pop-up chat invite from Julie.

JulieM467: George, are you on?

Again he hesitated. So many fakes. But then she was his only prospect at present. He typed a greeting before she disappeared.

GeorgeA405: I'm here, Julie. How are you?

JulieM467: Great. I got your message. Glad to hear you know what you're doing. That's kind of important. But why only fun, no strings? Are you married?

He chuckled. Savvy Julie.

GeorgeA405: No, are you?

JulieM467: I'm too busy to be married. I'm too busy for anything. I actually just got a new job. A second job.

GeorgeA405: What's your first job?

JulieM467: I can't really tell you. Not yet. So are you really safe? Or a maniac?

He chuckled again. He just might like this girl.

GeorgeA405: I can be a maniac. But I'm mostly sane. So are you really fit? Met with a girl who claimed to be fit but wasn't in any sense of the word. Can you e-mail a pic?

JulieM467: I don't have an anonymous e-mail for stuff like this. Can I post one through this site?

GeorgeA405: I don't think so. :(

JulieM467: I promise I'm fit. I'm in pretty good shape. What about you? Beer belly? Hillbilly teeth?

GeorgeA405: I do all right. Missing front tooth okay? The gap's not that big.

JulieM467: Hahaha. You're kidding, right?

GeorgeA405: Yes, no worries. I have all my teeth and more. Why don't we just meet? You seem fun. Of course you'll be a good girl and meet me somewhere public first. Well, somewhere public where we can talk privately.

He hit Send and held his breath. She would either say yes or no. She was either for real, or she was yanking him around. He hoped she was real. Her response took so long that disappointment set in, but then:

JulieM467: I know a place like that. An empty little café. How about coffee to start?

He thought about sitting through another awkward blind-date dinner.

GeorgeA405: Coffee sounds SPECTACULAR. Where is this empty little café you speak of?
JulieM467: It's uptown. It's on the same block as the Townsend Theater. Do you know where that is? It's just called Coffee Place. Silly name but the coffee is really good.

Jackson sucked in his breath and pushed back from the desk. His first impulse was to look around for cameras. His next impulse was to quickly log off. It might not be her. How could it possibly be her? It was just a coincidence.

No, it had to be her. On the heels of shock and horror came an intense impulse to try to engage her in impromptu cybersex. What perverse proclivities was his serious little ballerina hiding?

JulieM467: Are you still there?

GeorgeA405: I'm here. Just a minute. Googling your café. I'm actually in the same part of town.

JulieM467: Oh that's good. But it may be too tiny to be on Google.

GeorgeA405: No, I know it. It's beside a dry cleaners, right?

JulieM467: Yes, that's the place. Have you been there?

GeorgeA405: No.

The quick volley of messages halted for a moment. *You have to tell her. You can't just show up.* But if he told her, she wouldn't come. But if she did come, what would happen? How would she react? What would happen to their working relationship? His mind turned and argued against his will. *You shouldn't let this happen at all. You should log off and ignore all future messages from her.* But what he finally typed was:

GeorgeA405: Do you want to meet for coffee Sunday? Are you off your two jobs then?

JulieM467: <g> Yes, free from both jobs all day. What time? Noon?

He hoped he wouldn't live to regret it. He posted one last message.

GeorgeA405: Okay. Noonish at the Coffee Place. I'll recognize you by your red hair.

Prosper slept in Sunday morning after a night of tossing and turning. She got up and waxed. Bathed and pampered herself. She washed her hair and let it air-dry naturally so it curled up a little. She missed her curls, always straightened and smoothed into a bun. She was feeling curly today.

She'd logged on to the personals site last night after the performance and found a message waiting from George.

Looking forward to coffee tomorrow.
I'll be there right at noon. I'll be in a
blue shirt. I have blond hair that will
probably look messy. Still coming?

Messy blond hair. Why did she get so excited over that? She'd never been into messy hair until she met a certain choreographer. She'd written back:

Yes, still coming. I'll look for the guy
with the gap in his smile.

When she'd checked once more before bed, he'd written back:

It's really not that big. ;)

He was clearly funny and a great online flirt. But would they click in person? A few jokes about hillbilly teeth didn't mean they were made for each other. And this was such a blatant situation. When she'd met her last dom, it had begun slowly. It had developed as a normal relationship. In this case, it felt like meeting someone for the sole purpose of hooking up for sex. Maybe it only felt that way to her because she was so horny. Maybe this guy wasn't even after sex. Maybe he just wanted to tie her up and put clothespins all over her or something.

She hadn't wanted to ask for specifics while they messaged because a part of her was afraid to know. What if what he wanted wasn't what she wanted? *Must be sensual, crave training, accept pain.* That could describe a whole world of activities in BDSM. About his other words, *Play partner only, no commitment*, there could really be no misunderstanding. Well, the last thing she needed right now, with two jobs and a taxing ballet role, was a serious relationship.

Prosper made some mint tea and sipped it slowly, trying to calm her nerves. All she had to do was go to the coffee shop. They would talk. If things didn't feel right, well, she would leave. There was no reason at all to feel nervous. When it was almost eleven thirty, she started to get dressed. Against her better judgment, she put on sexy underthings. *Will you really go home with him?* Um...if he was fine enough, yes. It was very likely.

Black thong panties, black push-up bra. Garter belt with stockings. Tight-fitting black knit dress in order to make the most of what little she had. Some chunky patent pumps. Her black cardigan with gray embroidered flowers, and a black peacoat over the top. She left her hair down, frowning at it in the mirror. It wasn't the rich siren red most redophiles got off on. It was more like toxic orange. Oh well. She reminded herself that she had to prepare for him to reject her. She might be too thin, too short, not sexy enough. She didn't exactly exude sexuality. She put on some darkish lipstick and finished with some mascara and only light blush on her pale cheeks, because she knew she'd already blush more than enough.

She walked to the café, fighting down butterflies in her stomach. The chilly November day smelled of damp leaves and car exhaust. She stood outside the coffee shop just a moment, part of her wanting to dawdle, part of her afraid that he'd arrive and catch her shrinking outside. She took a deep breath and ducked inside, catching the door so the bells didn't jangle so loudly. The fresh scent of coffee and cinnamon replaced the dirty New York smell from outside. She scanned the deserted café, spotted the messy-blond-haired guy at the back.

Before she would really take him in, he turned in his chair, and she froze. Jackson looked her up and down with a half smile.

"Julie. You look almost exactly like another girl I know."

Chapter Four

"Prosper, wait."

He leaped up to go after her. She had her head tucked down, and her beautiful orange curls bobbed as she retreated at full speed. Her skirt swish-swished, and her little emo pumps clomped on the pavement. Even though his stride was longer, he had to run to catch up.

"Prosper, wait a minute, please." He pulled her into the first alcove they came to, which happened to be the stage door to the Townsend. He flicked his keys out of his pocket and unlocked it.

"No...I... No...Jackson...no..." She pulled away from him, shook her head even as he led her inside.

He backed her to the wall beside the door, trapping her there—not forcefully, but enough to make her still. "It's okay." He tried to sound calm and soothing. She stared at some point in the center of his chest. "I just want to talk to you. Let's talk, okay?"

It was dark backstage. The only light came from the red EXIT sign over their heads and the faint runner lights on the floorboards. He held her still, waiting for the flight response to subside. When he felt her relax under his fingers, he took her chin in his hand, tilted up her face, and kissed her. With an effort, he held his pelvis away from her, as much as he wanted to grind her against the wall. She pressed forward anyway, the flight response renewed, and then startled at the outline of his erection. She shrank back against the wall again. He trailed his fingertips across her cheek to gentle her and then kissed her again. This time she opened her lips a little. He could feel when she began to relax against him. Just as quickly, she pulled away.

"No," she whispered, shaking her head.

"Prosper." The pad of his thumb stroked her trembling chin. "It's okay. I'm not going to hurt you. I'm not going to do anything to you. Anything at all."

"You kissed me!"

"I barely kissed you." He held her still with the slightest pressure, just enough to cause her to submit. He looked at her lips and kissed her again, harder this time. It might be his only chance, so he intended to take advantage. She gasped into his mouth and struggled, flattening herself to the wall.

"Okay." He relented, releasing her. He backed up a foot or so and waited to see what would happen. A knee in the crotch? A frantic retreat out the door? But no, she only looked at him, no doubt shocked to find herself in his arms.

"Breathe," he said in a low voice. "Take some deep breaths before you pass out."

She stood rigid and dropped her gaze to the floor. He considered what to do. He had to say and do the right things. He had to play this precisely the right way. An hour from now, things would either be okay or not okay. Not okay would cause a world of problems for both of them.

He knew she was doing the same mental math. They would have to untangle things. He looked at her, watched her chest rising up and down. He'd never stood so close to her before, embraced her like this, when he wasn't leading her through some combination or dragging her across the rehearsal hall floor. She smelled like vanilla and brown sugar. He wanted to lick her. He wanted to eat her. All the things he'd never known about her before imprinted themselves on his mind. The smattering of barely visible freckles, the full red lips. The milky pale skin. Her sweet smell. The tentative way she'd responded to his kiss.

Her.

It can't be.

But it is.

He had been ridiculously specific in his personal ad. Fit, petite, red hair. He had described her exactly, wishing for her. Now she was standing in front of him, larger-than-life. The ad had produced the exact girl he wanted. Well, not exact. This wasn't exactly the girl he knew from rehearsal and class. She was made-up, dolled up in dark lipstick. Her hair, which he'd previously only seen rolled into severe or unruly buns, fell just past her shoulders in wild spiral curls of shiny orange spectacle. Instead of leotards and sweats, she had on a fitted black peacoat and a dress. But the beautiful face was utterly familiar.

"It's okay," he said. "All I'm asking you to do is talk. If you'd like, we can talk somewhere else, a restaurant or something."

She shook her head and swallowed hard. "No, I couldn't... No."

"Tell me why you're so upset."

She looked at him in disbelief, as if the answer should be obvious.

"Because...because...this is just..."

"Just what?"

"You knew." Her gaze accused him. "You knew it was me."

"No I didn't, not for sure. I suspected when you suggested this place. But I didn't really know. I could have asked, I suppose."

"Why didn't you?"

"Because if it was you, I didn't want to scare you off. Would you have come if you knew I was George?"

"Hell no! This is horrible. I actually think I'm going to die."

"Why, because now I know you're kinky? I knew all along."

Her mouth fell open in indignation. "You did not."

"I did too." He'd hoped she was, anyway, so it wasn't a total lie.

"Well, it doesn't matter," she said. "This is just—I can't—with you—"

"Oh, I'm quite certain you can." He leaned closer so his lips almost brushed against her ear. "This must be something you want very much to resort to meeting a stranger through an ad."

"I never should have done it," she said, shifting away from him. "I knew it was a mistake."

He restrained himself from touching the curls that rested on the delicate curve of her shoulder and ended just above the top button of her coat. He looked her over, checking for signs of availability and arousal. Her legs were still clamped shut, but her eyes were bright and feverish. Her chest rose and fell. Fear or excitement? He wondered if her nipples were hard. He wondered how well she would tolerate it if he tried to lead her further down the road she'd already chosen to take.

He had to try. He was quite capable of doing a scene that would have her all wrung out without touching her once. He could win her with words, and if his instincts were right, he could be touching her, really touching her, within the hour.

"Okay, Prosper. I'm going to speak frankly to you. First of all, I'm not embarrassed. Nor do I think this little encounter needs to change anything at all between us at the Townsend. I have no more or no less respect for you. Do you understand that, to begin with? Just answer yes or no."

"Yes."

"In fact, I'd very much prefer that what has happened here remain a complete secret."

"I want that too," she said with palpable relief.

"Okay, good. Now we've gotten that out of the way. Let's talk about what to do now. Obviously I'm a dominant male. You're a submissive female, from what I gather. Yes?"

She hesitated, then nodded.

"And surely you realize it was your attributes I described when I wrote that ad."

She nodded again.

"So it seems that's where we are. If fortune smiles, perhaps you found yourself, during rehearsals and class, attracted to me too?"

Her answering nod was slow to come and subtle, but the blush gave everything away.

"So the embarrassment, Prosper," he said. "Unnecessary. To me, this feels a lot more like good luck. Serendipity." He leaned an arm on either side of her head and pressed his front to her. "Relief."

She took a deep, shuddering breath just before his lips closed over hers. He marveled at the way she both melted to him and held herself away. Poor confused little submissive. He knew what to do with girls who needed guidance. He pulled back and stroked her cheek. "I know you're afraid. That's clear. But I think you're only afraid of the unknown. Are you inexperienced? You've never done this before?"

"Done what?"

"Exchanged power. Been someone's sub."

"Yes, I...I had a dom. A boyfriend." She waved her hand and grimaced.

"Didn't end well?"

She shook her head. "It didn't go very well from the beginning."

"Didn't know what he was doing?"

"I don't know. I guess he did."

"If you're only guessing, then no. He didn't know. Or he wasn't right for you."

The words hung in the air between them. The insinuation that he, Jackson, was. He remembered the feelings he got from watching her dance, watching her strive to reproduce his steps. Not just reproduce them but perform them perfectly every time. The concentration on her face, the furrowed brow, the small, tense lines at either side of her lips, the hyperalert eyes. She looked up at him that way now. She wanted to please him. She didn't know if she could, but he was pretty sure she wanted to try.

"Prosper..." He said her name on a long exhalation and shifted his knee forward between her legs. With only token resistance, her thighs parted, and he pinned her against the wall. His hands dropped to her waist, then he lifted her and pulled her close. They were eye to eye as his lips settled over hers once more. Her kiss was still tentative but less so this time. He cupped her jaw and slid one hand up into her nape, into the mass of copper orange hair that felt like velvet in his fingers. He made a sound, or maybe she did, as the kiss deepened with surprising intensity.

He backed away. They looked at each another. Her hands opened on his chest.

"But Jackson, what—how—"

"How will we face each other in the rehearsal room? We'll manage. We're consenting adults. A little discretion goes a long way."

He could see the wheels turning behind her green eyes.

"No, but…I mean…this will have to be a big secret. Work and this job, public and private relationships. And if I get attached to you—"

"We won't have to keep this secret very long. I leave in February, Prosper. Maybe March. So this only lasts until then. That's all I can offer you."

She fell silent and looked down. He knew that might be the end of it, but he had to warn her outright. He wasn't going to lead her on.

"So it will be our secret," she said.

"Yes. Our fun little secret for the next couple of months. Are you in or out, Prosper?"

She hesitated. "If I'm in, then what?"

"If you're in, I'd like you to come back with me to my place, strip down to your panties, and let me tie you to the bed." He crossed his arms over his chest and stared at her. "Wrists and ankles. Tied with rope."

She took a deep, shaky breath. "And then what?"

"That's all. I'll touch you a little. Talk to you. I won't keep you more than an hour, I swear."

"My last dom told me I should never let anyone tie me up the first time. That I needed to build trust first."

"I'm sure he had your best interests in mind when he said that. But do you really think we need to build trust? We've been rehearsing together for a month now."

She remembered lifts, balances. Hands that never once guided her the wrong way.

"But you won't...you won't..."

"Won't what? There are certain things I won't be able to do if your panties stay on."

He'd thought she was talking about sex, but she was clearly thinking of something else. He noticed the tense little lines around her mouth again.

"Pain. You're worried about pain? Whether I'm going to want to hurt you?"

She nodded.

"No, not this time. That's not something I do..." He almost said *at the start of a relationship*, but that was assuming things went well. She might run screaming from his place at any moment, and that would be that. Instead he said, "That's not something I do the first time I'm with somebody." An outright lie. If she'd been a regular girl, some anonymous, needy subby who'd answered his personal ad, he would have hurt her by this time already. Pinched her nipples, spanked her on the ass, pulled her head back by that luscious hair. But it was okay. Plenty of time to train her to more stringent play. She was a dancer. She would be able to handle the pain.

"I won't hurt you, not today, and I won't ask you to take off your panties. What's between your legs is not yet mine. Everything else I have a right to. Can you live with those terms for today? One hour?"

Not yet mine. The yet alarmed him. He already considered her his. Somehow he knew this was only the beginning; otherwise he would have pushed to have it all. Maybe he would still push to have it all when he got her alone. *No, no, don't go too fast. Don't scare her off.*

"What do you say?" he asked. "In or out?"

Please, please, please, Prosper. You can do this.

"In," she finally said.

5 Chapter Five

Prosper's fingers seemed to belong to another person as she unbuttoned her coat. She took a deep breath and shrugged out of it. Jackson hung it on a coatrack near the door while she looked around. His town house was sparsely furnished. A rental, obviously. One couch, one end table. One TV. One table between the living room and kitchen with a computer on it. One bar stool at the kitchen counter, and one coffee cup in front of it. Everything was neutral except for a large bowl of fruit on the counter and a colorful afghan over the arm of the couch. His apartment was very clean. She thought of her and Glenna's messy apartment. Thank goodness she hadn't taken him there. Not that she could have. What were they doing? What if someone found out about this? They would all assume she'd slept her way into Jackson's ballet.

Oh my God. He was looking at her.

"Come upstairs to the bedroom." She let him lead her across the living room and up to the second floor. His bedroom was as sparsely furnished as the rest of his house. A large iron bed dominated the room. There was a white shag rug on the floor and a bureau with a mirror across from the bed. She stood and watched with butterflies in her stomach as he folded down the white comforter.

"Down to your panties, Prosper."

She blinked, and then her fingers began to fumble with the zipper of her dress. Nudity wasn't a huge hang-up for her. Being a dancer, her body was always on display for appraisal and judgment. What made this different was that she was undressing for *him*.

He watched her from a few steps away. His burgeoning erection showed through the fabric of his pants. She couldn't look there, nor could she bear to look at his eyes, so she kept her gaze on the floor. She believed him when he said he wouldn't take what wasn't his. But the fact that his erection was there, blatantly obvious, made her own center throb and grow wet. She took off her dress and her bra, then looked down at her garter belt and stockings. Besides them, she wore only a teensy thong. She looked up at him, flushing hot.

"Yes, okay. Pretty lingerie. Leave it on."

With a sigh of relief, she went to the bed. By the time she'd arranged herself across the stark white sheets, he had equally stark white ropes dangling from his hand. He took first one wrist and then the other and tied them to the posts of the headboard with a casual ease that indicated he was far from new at this. They were soft ties, of nylon maybe, but they were strong. They had no give at all when she tested them with quick, furtive pulls. He watched her with a hint of a smile.

"You're caught now, aren't you? Try to get free. Pull hard."

She did and felt fearful excitement when she couldn't move her wrists more than an inch or two in each direction. He reached down and snapped one of her garters. She yelped at the sting and reached to soothe it, but her hand was stuck fast.

"Naughty girl. You wouldn't have worn those if you didn't have every intention of getting naked today with our friend George."

He looked down at her in mock censure. She shook her head.

"No, I wouldn't have. I only wore them... They make me feel... I hoped—"

He snapped the other garter. She yelped again and fidgeted on the soft sheets.

"Little liar."

"Really! If he... If you had been a stranger—"

"Stranger or not, Prosper, you should never let anyone tie you up unless you've negotiated first. You didn't even ask for a safe word."

"Safe word?"

He raised his eyebrows as he took her right ankle and pulled her legs apart.

"You are a novice." He wrapped her ankle in rope and secured it. "You don't know what a safe word is?"

"I know what a safe word is. But I know you. I trust you."

"What do you know about me? What do you know about my needs and my limits? Do they match yours?"

She looked at him, wrapping her mind around his questions. "I know you won't hurt me," she said finally.

"And how do you know that?"

"Because you need me for your ballet." He looked down at her and burst into laughter—a rich, warm sound she'd never heard before. She was so used to critical comments and serious commands that his laughter caught her off guard.

"Okay. You've got me there. Not that you're totally irreplaceable," he said, waggling a finger at her. She giggled at his teasing and felt herself relax. He wouldn't hurt her; she knew it. His fingertips brushed her ankle, checking the knot, making sure the rope was neither too loose nor too tight. The care he took made the warm throb intensify between her thighs.

"A common safe word partners use is *mercy*," he said. "Today we'll use that, not that you'll need a safe word. Just a formality."

She nodded as he walked to the other side of the bed to secure her left ankle. When he finished, she would be completely subdued, at his mercy. *Mercy*. It was an appropriate word, but it didn't feel safe. The fact that such a thing as a safe word needed to exist between them took her breath away.

He stood back when he finished, and his gaze swept over her, making her go hotter still. He looked like he knew exactly what he was doing, exactly what he wanted to do to her, and that made her wet, wetter than she could ever remember being. She was terrified he would touch her there and discover just how drenched she was.

"Okay?" he asked. "Your hands and feet feel okay? Your circulation isn't cut off? As you pointed out earlier, I have a bit of a vested interest in your body. If you feel anything going numb, let me know right away. Don't try to tough it out."

She nodded.

"You can answer 'yes, Sir.' The nods and headshakes seem a bit rude."

The reprimand in his tone washed over her, cold and hot lust. "Yes, Sir."

He sat beside her, his solid weight dipping the bed toward him. She stayed where she was, inexorably tied. He leaned close, so close she could smell him, the clean scent of soap and aftershave, an amalgamation of maleness. She breathed deep.

He lifted a lock of her hair and brushed it across her shoulder. "How do you feel, Prosper? Have you ever been tied up?"

She shook her head, then remembered and said, "No, Sir. Not like this. With rope instead of cuffs."

"Do you like it?"

His gaze penetrated her. There was no way to hide the truth from him.

"Yes."

"'Yes, Sir, I like it.'"

"Yes, Sir, I like it." Like it? She was so overwhelmed with arousal, she could barely get the words out.

"Speak so I can hear you. Talk to me when I ask you a question, no whispering."

"Yes, Sir, I like it." She managed to say it more loudly, but he must have heard her voice shake.

"Okay. Better." He reached a hand up to caress her jaw, the length of her neck, and down to the fullness of her breasts. She didn't know where to look. His eyes? His hand? His fingertips as they brushed across her nipples—*ohhhh*. She tried to hide her reaction to the stimulation, but a jerky breath escaped. His other hand came down next to her head, and he leaned forward over her and then drew the undisciplined little nipple into his mouth.

The sensation took her breath away. She writhed in the bonds, hating herself for doing it. He'd only been touching her for a minute, less than a minute, and already she was tossing around like a tart.

She tried to steel herself against the pleasure that threatened to undo her. With a smirk, he laved the other nipple, drawing it between rough lips that teased and tortured before releasing it with one sharp bite. She clenched her teeth to keep the groan inside. His fingertips touched the inside of her thigh and pinched her softly.

"Are you wet, Prosper?" He whispered it against her ear.

She closed her eyes. *Please don't touch me there, or you'll know. You'll know.*

"Answer me, 'yes, Sir' or 'no, Sir,'" he said. "Prosper, are you wet?"

"Yes, Sir," she whispered.

"Louder."

"Yes, Sir. I'm wet."

He moved his hand farther up the inside of her thigh, and she jerked again. He held his palm over the inadequate triangle of material that covered her. It hovered there, a hairbreadth away. If he pressed down, his palm would come away soaking wet.

"Please—"

His unforgiving gaze was terrifying. "Please what? Please touch you?"

"No, no," she pleaded. "Please don't."

"I already know you're wet." He smiled. "You told me. Either way I would have known. I can look at your eyes and see it."

"I just don't want you to—"

"Take it as an invitation?"

"It's just my body, my body doing things—"

"Your mind doesn't agree with your body? Your mind isn't turned on by what I'm doing to you? Tying you down, touching you, but not quite touching you enough?"

She looked at him, desperately wanting to produce the right answer. In the end she kept silent, too horny to speak.

"I turn you on because I like to see it. I'd like to feel it too, but I won't. Not today. But if I'm turning you on, don't try to hide it from me. Do you understand, girl?"

Her mouth fell open a little. If he made her any hotter, her pussy was going to set fire to his bed.

"'Yes, Sir,'" he prompted her.

"Yes, Sir, I won't hide it. I—I'll try not to—"

"Try? No. See that you do."

He moved his hand up the inside of her thigh slowly, teasingly. "Okay. Let's go again. Show me how it feels."

When his palm hovered over her center, when she couldn't evade his eyes and she felt she would die from craving his touch, she stretched and arched with a soft sigh.

"Good girl," he said. "More." He lowered his mouth to her nipples again and wrested two throaty moans from her as he pulled each one into his mouth and suckled it. Her chest rose and fell as pleasure flooded her.

"You're beautiful like this," he whispered. "Under my power. Under my control. Do you want me to control you, Prosper?"

"Oh, yes, Sir." She said the words with no conscious thought, only knowing they were true.

"And what if it hurts sometimes? Will you still want it?"

"Yes. Yes..." His hand was running over her belly now, down over her garter belt, then lower. He pressed just where her thong began, at the top of her pubis. She gritted her teeth and strained at the ropes. *Lower, lower! Please!*

"Yes, I see now." His breath blew against her ear. "I see exactly what you need. Exactly what you want."

She shook her head, past rational thought. He was torturing her. The heel of his hand pressed again on her pubic bone but slid no lower. It wasn't enough; it wasn't enough!

Then his hand left her. He rolled off the bed and began to untie her ankles. Her hips arched, seeking fulfillment he wasn't going to give. "Our hour is almost up," he said.

No, no, it can't be. I need more.

He untied her other ankle, then knelt over her to untie her wrists. He straddled her naked breasts, and she could feel his knees pressed against her shoulders, the rough fabric of his pants chafing her nipples. His erection, though clothed, thrust practically against her face. She felt pinned. She felt completely submissive to him. Prosper had never in her twenty-five years wanted to suck a man's cock, but she thought if he weren't dressed, that's exactly what she would have done. She would have opened her mouth and taken his full length gratefully. She would have had no choice from the way his body subdued her, and that turned her on most of all.

When her wrists were untied, he moved aside and leaned down to kiss her. "Turn over," he said against her jaw. And then when she hesitated, "Just obey. I've already told you I won't hurt you."

She turned over, and when she was on her belly, he knelt between her legs and pushed her thighs wider apart. She felt the impulse to resist him, but he made a noise in his throat, and she yielded.

"I'm not going to tie you this time. Put your hands over your head. Hold the headboard. Stay that way."

She did as she was told. He ran his hands up her back, warm, rough contact, then snaked them around and underneath to grope her breasts. She arched, trying to draw her legs together, but his knees were impeding her, spreading her wide. She lay still instead, taking short, panicked breaths like a trapped animal. *He won't hurt you. He won't hurt you.*

But that wasn't why she trembled. No. It wasn't pain she feared. It was something she wanted, something so overwhelming she could barely control herself. She ground against the coverlet, felt the silk triangle of fabric adhere to the wetness between her legs. She tried to ease the ache building there, but he made a noise of disapproval. He put his hands around her waist and stilled her, preventing her attempt at relief. "No. I'm in charge right now, not you."

She moaned—a fervent, desperate sound she couldn't believe had come from her own lips.

He didn't relent. "No. I said no."

He rubbed the small of her back with his thumbs. His hands were large enough to almost completely span her waist. The hard grip reminded her of the way he partnered her in rehearsals. His touch then had hinted at a power, a ruthless ability she didn't understand.

She understood it now.

She went pliant under his hands, gave herself up to his mastery. Her past D/s experiences had been nothing like this. She felt, for the first time, truly dominated. She was at his mercy. She shivered and tensed, resisting the urge to let go of the headboard and soothe the part of her that ached.

He shifted behind her and moved closer. He drew one hand up the inside of her thigh, the other arm wrapped under her hips, cradling her, or perhaps holding her so she couldn't get away. His palm hovered, lingered over her hot, aching center. Oh, he was going to touch her!

"Don't move. Not one inch."

Oh God, she was going to die. She felt the heat of his palm where he held it still over her pussy. If he didn't touch her, if he didn't plunge his fingers inside—It took every fiber of her control not to arch forward against his palm. She vibrated under his fingers, craving, needing satisfaction. If only he would touch her—

"Good girl," he said, releasing her. "Time's up."

6 CHAPTER SIX

She pulled on her clothes, blushing and coy again the moment the naughty lingerie was hidden underneath. He watched her dress with a mixture of wonder and depression. He squelched the urge to strip her naked again and take her down to the bed. His fantasies of a raunchy, sex-soaked romp with Julie were long forgotten. His chaste little scene with Prosper had been much better than anything he could have dreamed.

He hadn't slept with her, they hadn't had intercourse, but he'd touched every part of her he'd longed to touch since he first watched her take class. Well, he hadn't touched *every* part of her, but close enough. Close enough to hold him until the next time. There would be a next time; that was sure. He hadn't asked her about it because he wouldn't leave it up to her. No, her first instinct would be to run away, to create safe distance. He wouldn't leave the decision with her.

When she was ready, Jackson walked her back to her apartment. He was alert for troubled signals, impending hysteria, but she seemed strangely calm. She didn't talk, and he chose not to press her into conversation. He assumed that, like him, she was still working through what they'd just done.

He pulled her close in the stairwell outside her apartment and brushed a quick kiss against her ear. "Okay, Prosper?"

She nodded. He looked down at her.

"What's wrong?"

"We didn't do much negotiating, did we? Much talking?"

"We talked enough," he said. "I learned some things about you."

Her blush was delicious. He wanted to lick it right off her face. He settled for another lingering kiss. "Prosper..." His tongue glided across her lips. He took her head in his hands and kissed her more deeply. He felt her grasp at his arms for balance and, without thinking, shifted to compensate. Once a partner, always a partner. Is that why he felt he already knew this girl inside and out? Because he'd danced with her? He pulled away, unbalanced by the sudden rush of possession he felt. *No strings...*

"Okay," he said. "I guess I'll see you tomorrow after class."

She opened her mouth, then shut it. He thought perhaps she was unsure whether to answer *yes, Sir* or simply call him Jackson again.

"'Sure, Jackson' is perfectly fine now."

"Sure, Jackson," she said. "See you at rehearsal."

"Do you have your key?"

She fumbled in her bag for it. Before she could unlock the door, he took her arm and leaned close, his lips at her ear.

"One more thing I forgot to tell you. You may not touch yourself. At all. No masturbation, no orgasms until we're together again. When I see you, I'll know."

Her beautiful mouth gaped. He gave her elbow one last squeeze and left her on her doorstep.

He walked back to his place slowly, basking in the afterglow of a highly satisfying afternoon. He went straight upstairs and collapsed facedown on the bed. Her perfume, the smell of her hair, the primal fragrance of her center was in the bedding. Like a predator, he already knew her by scent. He turned over and stared at the ceiling, daydreaming about black stockings, straining hips, and fiery orange hair.

"Prosper!" Glenna ambushed her as soon as she shut the door behind her. "What are you all dressed up for? You were out with someone? A guy?"

She shrugged. "We just met for coffee."

"Who is he? Do I know him? Where did you meet?"

"Um...well..." She wished she had prepared some kind of story in advance.

"Is he a dancer?"

Prosper coughed. "Well, um...no."

"Is he cute? What's his name?"

"His name is J-John. And he was cute, yeah. It was kind of a blind-date thing."

"What did you do?"

"Um, we mostly talked and had coffee. We'll see where it goes."

"God, you look so cute. I love those shoes. I'm sure he liked you. Damn, I'm so jealous of your hair! I love it curly like that!"

Glenna went on awhile longer, until Prosper managed to excuse herself. The rest of the day was a complete waste. All she could do was think about him, the things he'd said, the things he'd done to her. That night she tossed and turned, remembering every moment, from the time he'd turned to her in the coffee shop and shocked her senseless to the time he'd kissed her outside her apartment door. *You may not touch yourself.* Her fingers curled into tight fists, trying to resist. He had awakened new sensations, new vistas inside her that she hadn't even known existed. All her past sexual experiences paled in comparison to her interlude with Jackson, and he hadn't even fucked her. She placed her hand between her thighs the way he had, hovering just over her hot, slick core. She arched and squirmed, desperate to contact her aching clit but at the same time knowing she didn't dare.

Why not? Because he'd told her not to? Did she owe him obedience like that? Did she have to allow him to control her?

No, she didn't have to, but she wanted to. Every moment she lay in bed trying not to fondle herself, her mind fixated on him. He might as well have been lying right beside her, staring a warning at her. She could still feel the tensile fingers, the broad, warm hands. The rough lips against her earlobe. She would see him the next morning after class. He would know. She had to do as she'd been told.

But it was so hard not to touch herself, to try to soothe the ache. She pressed her legs together, turned, and sighed, and when morning dawned, she'd hardly managed any sleep.

He didn't have to turn to know when she was standing in the door to the rehearsal room. Her soft footsteps alerted him, the bright flash of hair in the mirror. *Keep it together, Jack.* He could already feel his cock rising, and he hadn't even turned to her yet.

Dammit.

He sat by the wall, held his dance book in his lap, ignoring her with everything he was worth. He wondered how she'd looked at him when she'd entered. Shyness? A smile?

He heard soft murmurs of greeting between her and Blake, saw her begin to stretch at the barre—again, from under his lashes. He would never survive this. *Focus. Work is work, play is play.*

For a moment he actually considered sending them home, canceling practice, but that was impossible. He looked up at her finally, and she turned her back on him with a frown. What did she want him to do, acknowledge what had happened between them last night? Here? Now? In front of Blake?

"Let's begin with the capture," Jackson said. "From the top."

The dancers moved through the sequence. They were really improving as partners. Blake was getting used to her smaller, lighter stature, and she was relaxing into his grip. He made them repeat the steps two, three times, added more, tried newer, more intricate combinations they both struggled with but eventually achieved.

He stood and moved nearer to his Firebird and tried very hard not to remember her as she had been the night before. It wasn't difficult. The silent girl before him in a light pink leotard and tights bore no resemblance to the black-stockinged siren of last night. Her frown was exhausting, though. He finally stopped looking at it. When an hour had passed, he let them go.

She skittered from the room, head down, those tiny tension lines all around her mouth. He could have gone after her, called her back. He could have pulled her close and whispered in her ear, *Did you touch yourself last night? Or did you obey me?*

But there was no reason to ask if she'd obeyed him, because he knew with absolute certainty that she had. He wasn't even into orgasm denial, not really. In fact, if he got his wish, he would be making her come up and down and sideways—and soon. No, it was an exercise, a test. A way to gauge if she was going to cooperate, if she was invested. If she would obey him when the things he asked for were hard. He knew she had a strong drive to please, a drive to receive approval. He could use that to suit his own purposes very well.

So Jackson didn't go after her. Such behavior would draw attention. There were dancers all around, and dancers gossiped hard. He did stay for the show to watch Prosper from the seats. He went backstage for the second half but didn't see her. He'd intended to talk to her, reassure her that his cool demeanor during rehearsal was only to keep their secret safe. But instead of Prosper, he ran into Lawrence, who grilled him on the new *Firebird*. Yes, he would start rehearsing with the corps soon. Yes, Prosper Ware was turning out quite well.

"Such a surprise sometimes," Lawrence said. "What they have inside them."

Jackson nodded. *Tell me about it.* "You know what they say, Lawrence. It's always the quiet ones."

"Just so," he agreed. "And how is she doing with Blake? Good partnership?"

"Yes. They're finally starting to get comfortable."

Lawrence paused. "Kristen is making noises about going to another company. Do you think Prosper will expect to move to principal permanently?"

"Don't you want her to?"

"I don't know. I hate to lose Kristen, but if you think Prosper is principal material..."

"She's definitely principal material." He looked hard at Lawrence. "Is it only her small size that you don't like?"

"She's just so serious in her focus." Lawrence shook his head so his white-gray hair fell into his eyes. "Almost joyless in a way."

"A small price to pay for perfect dancing," Jackson said. "When you watch her Firebird, you'll see."

Tuesday after class Prosper dawdled, stretching and rubbing her legs.

"Tired from all your prima ballerina dancing?" Glenna teased.

"No," she said. "Just basically tired."

And she was tired. Prosper hadn't been able to sleep last night again, this time not from sexual frustration but from ire. Yes, they'd said no strings, but how dare he just totally ignore her? As if nothing had taken place between them at all? And now she was off to suffer the same indignity again. She was waiting outside the rehearsal room as the other dancers filed in, not quite ready to face Jackson yet, when Blake loped up to her side.

"Prosper. Hey."

The southern lilt to his voice always surprised her, at odds with his ethnic face. "Hi, Blake."

She wondered what was going on. Even after weeks of rehearsals, he hadn't deigned to speak to her outside of short exchanges required by their *Firebird* parts.

"Company rehearsals today. Excited?"

She shrugged. "I guess."

"It's good. When they see what you're doing, what Jackson's been doing—"

"They've already seen it." What did he think would change? They'd been watching through the windows for weeks, had already seen Jackson berating her, seen her trying to capture the choreography with debatable success.

"Listen, Prosper, maybe you don't want to hear this. Maybe you hate me, maybe you don't want my advice, but I'm going to say it anyway. You're a talented dancer. You know what you're doing, and you could be promoted to principal soon. You should lighten up a little."

She moved to leave, but he blocked her and backed her against the wall. She was about to shove him away when she looked to the side and saw Jackson turn and disappear into the rehearsal space. Had he seen Blake cornering her there, leaning in for what could have been a kiss but was only a lecture?

"You need to learn to network," Blake said. "The world of dance is social. Why don't you try cracking a smile every once in a while?"

"I smile all the time. I'm perfectly happy. But I'm not going to act fake and schmooze and pretend to like your nasty friends."

"Those friends can get you places—places you can't get by yourself. Or are you depending on your other *friend*?" They both knew exactly who he meant. "Do you think he's going to do anything for you once this is all done? I'm sure this is what he does, over and over. Picks a ballerina he likes. Uses her and loses her. Moves on when the inspiration is gone. You're not sleeping with him, are you? Jesus, tell me you're not."

She looked up at her partner, then pushed him away. "Thanks for your concern and advice, but I don't really need it. I know what you and your friends think of me. I know what people are saying. I don't care. All I care about is getting this ballet perfect. So just partner me, Blake, and shut the fuck up."

Jackson ground his teeth as the dancers began to file in for practice. He was still trying to erase the image of Blake leaning over his Prosper in the hallway. *His* Prosper. Was she his? Blake was no fool. He probably sensed the passion beneath Prosper's demure exterior. It had been a punch in the gut, seeing them together. For all he knew, they'd been hooking up for weeks. It wasn't unheard of. It was quite common, actually, for romance to flower between ballet partners.

He groaned inwardly. No. He could bear not having her, but he couldn't bear watching Blake paw at her in the halls. No.

They entered separately. He watched them. They didn't interact like people in a relationship. Of course he and Prosper didn't interact like people in a relationship either. If Blake and Prosper were together, they'd hide it. The very idea of it filled him with rage, the idea of Blake's hands all over her perfectly sculpted body, her sensitive flesh.

Focus.

It was the first day of rehearsals with the corps, so they were in the big practice room. Even so, it felt crowded. He missed practicing alone with her, although it was easy enough to keep track of her among the other dancers. He just had to look for her hair. They worked on the second act, the frenetic dance when the Firebird drove Kostchei's minions to dance until they died. In Fokine's version, they didn't die but only fell asleep. Jackson decided he wanted Prosper to leave behind a stage full of corpses. By the end of the ninety-minute rehearsal, the corps, who had never worked with Jackson before, feared his awful wrath. Any poor corps dancer who found himself out of step or not paying attention was the victim of a vicious harangue. But he was hardest on Prosper.

"Faster, faster!" He drove her, even when he knew she was doing her best. "Move your feet! You're supposed to be flying!"

"Okay!"

"No. Like this..." He marked the beats with sharp claps, but she couldn't match his tempo. He grew more frustrated, pounded the rhythm with his fist in his palm.

"I'm trying!" She fell off pointe and spun on him. "What do you want from me? I'm giving you my best, everything I have! If it's not good enough for you—" She threw her arms up and stalked away to lean against the barre.

He blew out his breath and looked around at the corps. All of them watching.

"Okay. Enough for today. Thank you. We'll pick up here tomorrow."

The dancers left quickly, not waiting around to socialize or deconstruct the rehearsal with their friends. They scattered like roaches under a spotlight.

All of them but her.

He grabbed his dance book and his bag and headed to the door to find her standing alone there in the corner, glaring at him. It was a private place to stand, a place the other dancers couldn't see even looking in windows. He closed the door and turned to her.

"Very professional."

"Right back at you."

"Are you seeing him?" he blurted out before he could stop himself.

"Who?" The confusion on her face made the knot inside him relax. She wasn't capable of subterfuge.

"Blake," he said anyway. "Tell me the truth."

"No, of course I'm not seeing him." She shook her head and turned away, shouldering her dance bag. His hand closed around her arm. "Let go of me," she said tightly.

He released her and bowed his head to hers. "Okay. For now. But I will touch you eventually. And you won't be the one giving orders then." He held himself a body's width apart from her. "They're watching, Prosper. Always. You wanted discretion."

"I know. And I don't care. I don't have time for this anyway. For you. To see you. So I don't care—I'm busy, and I'm concentrating on this ballet, so—" She wouldn't meet his eyes. "I mean, whatever. If you're over it, I don't care."

"You think I'm over it? Because I want to work and not play flirty goo-goo eyes with you? We agreed, you and I, that we would not bring it here. You seemed very relieved when I suggested it, if I remember correctly. You're my dancer here. Not my girlfriend, not my—" He fell silent.

"Fuck buddy?" she supplied in a voice edged with sarcasm.

"Okay," he said. "Just take some deep breaths."

"I don't want to take deep breaths. I don't want you to tell me what to do."

"I think you do want it. You're just upset because you think I'm pushing you away." He dropped his voice lower. "The truth is, I wish I could take you in my arms right now. I wish I could rip that fucking leotard off you and take you to the floor, and I can't even put into words what I'd like to do to you then."

She didn't look at him, but she was suddenly taking those deep breaths he'd urged her to take.

"Believe me, Prosper, I find this just as awful as you do. But we will not bring this here again. We can't work and keep our places in this company if the nature of our relationship was exposed. And yes, little one"—he leaned closer—"we do have a relationship, you and me. Fuck buddy doesn't quite describe it."

She didn't speak for a long while.

He couldn't read her. "Are you okay?"

She let out a sharp little breath. "Yes. I'm okay. I'm a little..." She fell silent.

"Angry? Confused? Scared?"

"Horny. Can I touch myself tonight?"

He blinked and chuckled. Not what he'd expected. "'May I touch myself, Sir?' would be a better way to ask."

"May I touch myself, Sir?" Her barely concealed pique made his cock twitch.

"No. Absolutely not. You can only come when I make you come."

"But—"

"But what?"

"That's not fair to get me all worked up and then not let me relieve myself!"

"Life's not fair, girl. Not for subs like you. Here. Give me your cell phone."

She dug in her bag and got it out. He programmed his number into it, then handed it back to her.

"If it gets too hard not to touch yourself, you're welcome to call me and beg. Not that it will do any good."

Prosper tsked in annoyance, clearly not finding the situation as amusing as he did. She dug her toes into the floor. "It's hard not to masturbate when I feel so...so..."

"Horny?"

"Yes. I mean, are you going to have sex with me?"

"You bet your fucking feathers I am, Firebird. Soon."

"Well, um...when?" She looked ridiculously adorable begging him for sex.

"How about tonight?"

"I have to work tonight."

"Oh yes, your second job. Where?"

"At Halo. That bar."

He hated the idea of her working in a skin bar like Halo, not that it was any of his business.

"I'm not working tomorrow night," she said.

Tomorrow night. He was going to fuck her to pieces.

"Fine," he said. "Tomorrow night after the show. At my place."

CHAPTER SEVEN

Wednesday night she climbed into a cab wearing the clothing he'd instructed her to. Tight black dress with a gartered corset and stockings under it, no panties. Yeah. She was a slut.

But she was an excited slut. She shifted on the backseat of the cab, already growing damp between her legs. It wasn't just the way she was dressed. It was the knowledge that she was going to Jackson's home to have sex. They'd made a date. For sex. Arrangements to fuck. It was so hedonistic. He wanted to penetrate her, touch her in all her most private places. And she desperately wanted to be touched by him.

She pressed her legs together, watching the people out on the street. She wanted to roll down the window and shout out her happiness. Finally everything was coming together for her. She had her part-time job nailed down, and just that morning she'd finally located a studio apartment she could rent week to week for a reasonable rate. And now she was on the way to Jackson's house for *sex*. He was going to put his hands on her, press his hard, powerful body against hers. He was going to penetrate her with the cock she'd seen straining in his pants, the cock she couldn't stop obsessing about. Oh my God. She arrived five minutes early and sat in the cab a full minute or two gathering her nerves.

"Everything all right?" the driver asked.

"Everything's great." She handed him the money Jackson had given her for the short cab ride. *Take a cab. I don't want you walking without panties after dark.* It was a generous tip, and the driver thanked her, then got out to open her door. As she stepped out in her tight dress, cold air blew up to caress her naked flesh. She shivered and ran up the stairs, then pressed the buzzer for Jackson's townhome.

The door swung open, and there he was. He pulled her inside, no words, no smile. He pushed her back against the door as it closed and locked the dead bolt with a click. Her indrawn breath sounded loud in the silence. The lights were low, and his face as she looked up at it was shadowed. Without preamble, he stuck his hand up her dress. He felt the top of her stockings, the garters. His hand cupped her naked sex, and then he bent down and kissed her forehead.

"Good girl."

She was so hot, so wet. His fingers grazed her, felt the slick nectar there. He wanted to thrust his fingers up inside her until she went up on her toes, but he wasn't going to maul her thirty seconds in. No. He wouldn't maul her yet.

His face was inches from hers. She looked up at him with a wide-eyed gaze that made his erection throb. He leaned against her so she could feel it against her belly. She quivered like a spooked sparrow trapped between him and the wall. He was her cage. He held her captured and still; she didn't make the smallest attempt to get away. But what would he do with her now? The possibilities were endless. There were so many things he wanted to do to her that he didn't know where to begin.

So he held her trapped while he grasped for control. He could feel the heat radiating from her. He wanted to push her to the floor, yank her dress up. Force himself inside, ride her hard. What would she do? How would she react? Would she struggle and pull away? Would she spread her thighs wider, let him sink in where he so desperately wanted to be? What kind of sounds would she make? Squeaks of fear, guttural moans? Urgent gasps?

"I want to fuck you, Prosper."

Okay. Not exactly a love sonnet. She swallowed, took a shuddery breath.

"I want to fuck you," he repeated. "I need sex from you."

"Okay. I better warn you, though, I'm not that good at sex."

"Aren't you?" The very idea was ridiculous, but she seemed to believe it. "Are you at least good at sucking cock?"

His words brought a flush to her cheeks.

"I'm...I'm terrible at it...Sir."

A moment of utter silence. Then he laughed.

"Honest to a fault. Your name should be Honesty, not Prosperity. So you're not good in bed at all?"

Prosper bit her lip, then shook her head.

"One more head shake and I'll spank your ass until it's black-and-blue." He took her chin hard in his hand, tilting her face up. "Your skill in bed aside, do you want me? Are you hot for me? Are you wet?"

She nodded, then remembered and spit out a "yes, Sir," but he was already propelling her toward the couch. Her gasp was muffled by the cushions as he bent her over the arm. He yanked up the skirt of her dress, then tore off his belt and doubled it over in his hand. She squealed and jerked as the first blow landed.

"I'm sorry! Ow! I forgot!"

She kicked her legs as he brought the leather belt down on her ass again. Her distressed yelps and jerks excited the sadist in him. Her ass cheeks clenched as she tried to twist away from the pain. Three vivid stripes of red. He drew back and landed a fourth stroke on her gorgeous bottom.

"Please! Please, Sir—" He noted her distress but continued the punishment with a couple more heavily placed blows. Even without her head-shaking issues, he would have spanked her before he fucked her. She would be in the space he wanted that way, the submissive, pain-evasive state where she would do whatever he asked.

"Hush. Keep the noise down," he said as her sobs and wails escalated. "I'll gag you if you don't."

She buried her face in the cushions and made muffled keening sounds that aroused him so much he gave her four more licks instead of two. When her bottom looked sufficiently red, he dropped the belt on the sofa cushion next to her face.

"Kiss it, and thank me for correcting you."

She did as she was told, sniffling and snuffling. He released her and pulled her upright. Her small body quailed in his hands, made him feel even more powerful and drunk with lust.

"Now I want you to look at me and tell me exactly what you're feeling. Take a moment if you need time to figure out what to say."

"I feel sorry. And punished." Her fingers toyed with the skirt of her dress, still pulled up around her waist. "I feel scared of you a little. That really hurt."

"It was supposed to hurt. And you're supposed to be a little scared of me. It's best that way, isn't it?"

His fingers trailed up to find the zipper on the back of her dress. He drew it down and took the dress off her, so she stood before him in her corset and stockings. He turned her around, admiring her. The sight of her spanked ass and naked pussy drew him with a magnetic pull. His fingers slipped between her legs, probed her there. He felt slight resistance and tightened his grip on her. He sighed as he discovered the hot moisture within her folds.

"Yes, you see. You like being scared. And you love being hurt." He brought his fingers to her lips. "Suck. Practice for what comes next."

She hesitated, opened her mouth. Her tongue caressed his fingers in delicate licks at first, then stronger strokes. He made an encouraging sound, and she started to suck.

His whole body went rigid. He was going to explode if he didn't get inside her. It would take three rounds at least to get to a point where he could think again. For now, lust ruled. He pulled out the condom he'd pocketed earlier, then tore his clothes off. "Kneel down. Open your mouth."

"Okay, but I don't really know how—"

"Just open your mouth. Open wide." He rolled on the condom. He was as hard as he'd ever been in his life. He guided the head of his cock to her mouth, then slid it between her lips. "Good girl," he said as she began gingerly licking and sucking. He wanted to bury himself in the back of her throat, but it was far too soon for that. Instead he basked in her earnest attempts to please him, the inexperienced but effective movements of her tongue around the sensitive head of his dick. "Take me deeper." He pressed forward and felt her tongue lick down the front of his shaft. He let out a long gasp that turned into a groan.

He put his hands on her head, one wrapping around to cup the back of her neck. Close control was something he would need to get her used to for future instruction. *Future instruction.* The idea of it made him jerk and swell in her mouth.

She stopped, pulled back a little. He loosened his hold. "Don't stop."

"Am I... Is it okay? Does it feel good?"

"The fact that your mouth is filled with my hard cock should be a signal to you that things are going well. Stopping to talk is not a good thing." He took her chin in his hand and nudged inside her mouth again. God, the tentative, messy blowjob was the best he'd ever had. Her clumsy attempts to caress and explore him with her tongue were sexier to him than the most skilled courtesan's oral gymnastics. His whole body grew tense with hot pleasure, and she gagged slightly as he nudged deeper into her mouth.

"You're inexperienced, I know." He thrilled at the sight of his cock sliding in and out of her lovely red lips. "Practice will help."

He twisted her hair in his fingers and gritted his teeth, delaying his orgasm. He wanted to enjoy every last moment of possession.

Finally he couldn't hold off anymore. "Okay, girl. Jesus." He grunted, holding her hair hard and thrusting deep as he came. All his fantasies and yearnings came to shuddering fruition as the orgasm overtook him. He was aware of the heat of her mouth, the softness of her hair under his touch, every aspect of the long-awaited sexual release. His legs trembled from the intense, expulsive shock of climax that emanated from his cock and balls to every part of his body. As the groan died away in his throat, she began to pull away.

"Wait. When I say."

She froze, holding his still-pulsing dick in her mouth. He pulled away finally but kept her chin cupped in his hand. He looked down at her as he slipped off the condom.

"Okay. God. Now that that's taken care of, I can think straight again. Let's sit for a minute and have a drink."

Foolish of her. When he'd said, "Let's sit for a minute and have a drink," she had imagined actually sitting somewhere, perhaps on the plush textured sofa he'd just beaten her over, or at the table over by the kitchen. But no. She was tied spread-eagle to his iron headboard and footboard while he had a drink and occasionally had her lick some drops from his fingers. She wasn't much of a drinker, so she didn't know what it was, and she was too mindless with lust to ask.

She had never in her life given a successful blowjob. She'd tried, but invariably the guys had stopped her, given up, and decided to try to come another way. Honestly, her heart had never been in it. She'd thought it gross, icky. Dirty. Well, she had before. Obviously she felt differently now. She had sucked him off eagerly and enjoyed every moment of it, driven on by his insistent hands in her hair.

She looked at him now, and he gazed back at her with a lazy smile. She looked away, blushing. He dipped his fingers into the amber liquid for her to suck on, then brought an ice cube to her lips. "Hot, girl?"

Damn it. She was burning, while he was calm and satisfied. The agitation, the intensity he'd greeted her with had disappeared with his convulsive orgasm. Now she was the one who was agitated, while he seemed perfectly content to play.

"Lick it nicely," he chided when she tried to bite the cube he held to her mouth. "Toy with it like you toyed with my cock before."

Half-embarrassed, half-aroused, she tongued it, using the tip to swirl around one pointed end of the cube. She opened wider, stuck her tongue out, and lapped at the broad icy surface.

"Mmm, that's right. Very fast learner. Inborn talent. But I knew that already about you." He replaced the cube in the glass and looked down at her, tracing his finger along the stays of her corset. "I bet your mother was a siren, wasn't she? A total slut."

"My mother was Amish."

Jackson did an exaggerated spit take that started her giggling.

"I know—it's weird. She's not anymore. They shunned her when I was just a baby."

"Why?"

"It came out that I...I wasn't my father's daughter."

She saw understanding dawn. He reached for a lock of her hair.

"Next-door neighbor was a redhead?"

"Something like that. My mother and the man she had...sinned with...were driven away. But he went back to the People before long. He left her, and they took him back. My mother married again and..."

She waved her hand. Jackson played with her locks, twirling the curls around his fingers.

"I can't imagine hiding this hair of yours away under one of those staid white caps. Criminal. Thank God she didn't return when he did. You'd be sitting somewhere reading a Bible right now."

She shrugged. "It was never the life for my mother. She was a dancer too. Well, she wanted to be. When she was little, she would hide away and dance in secret because it wasn't permitted. She had to make up her own songs to dance to. She was a free spirit, though, all her life. When I started to dance, I was very little. Two or three. She was overjoyed."

She fell silent. He looked at her expectantly, but she didn't go on. He took another drink, and while she wanted his fingers in her mouth again, he gave her more questions instead.

"You said she was. Is she still alive?"

"Oh yes. She is."

"Still overjoyed that you dance?"

"I guess. I don't see her very much." Her voice wobbled. She felt the familiar agitation that overcame her whenever she talked about her mother, her family. She knew he noticed, but mercifully he let that line of questioning drop.

"So Prosperity is Amish in origin, I suppose?" He drained the last of the drink and then set it on the table beside the bed. She watched the muscles of his stomach shift and contract as he bent and straightened, watched the perfection of his outstretched arm, his wrist, his hand. He resumed his seat between her thighs, pinching the tender skin above her stocking.

"Answer me."

"No, Sir," she said, tearing her gaze from his thickening cock. "My Amish name was Mary. My mother changed it after she left."

"In a fit of optimism for her new life?"

"Yes. Maybe. I don't know." She was finding it hard to concentrate on the conversation as his hands ran up both her thighs. She tried hard to be still, to not buck and fidget the way she wanted to. She wanted to lift her hips and thrust her throbbing clit right against his hand. *Please touch me; please touch me; please touch...*

"Hot, Prosper?" He knelt over her so his eyes were inches away. His expression demanded an answer.

"Yes, Sir."

"'Yes, Sir, I'm hot,'" he prompted.

"Yes, Sir. I'm hot." She practically whimpered the words.

"I can see that you are." He moved one hand to her breast, pulled the cup of the corset down so her nipple was exposed, taut and pointed. "Hot indeed." His fingertips brushed across her nipple, making her breath stop. With each light stroke, the fire in her clit flared. Then the fingertips clamped down, hard, harder, twisting. The pain became excruciating, shocking. Her plaintive groan rose to a cry. "Ohhh! Please!"

"Shh. I'm just getting started with you. You're not very good at sex, remember? I think I'll need to work on conditioning some appropriate sexual response." As he spoke, his fingertips moved to torture her other rock-hard nipple. Then he took both firmly between the pads of his thumbs and forefingers and squeezed.

Oh God! The pain in her nipples and the throbbing in her pussy became one crippling ache. She needed more; she needed less. He was making her lose her mind. She panted, throwing her head back.

"You seem to like that well enough." He released her and slid one cool palm down the length of her smooth black corset to where her hips arched, searching for contact, searching for release. "Let's see how you like this." His palm stroked over her mons and stopped, one dexterous fingertip brushing once, twice across her clit. She gasped and strained at the bonds.

"Please!"

"Please, what?"

"Please, again! Please, again, Sir!"

He pretended to consider it. "Okay. First I want to hear you say you like sex."

"I like sex!" she babbled immediately.

"'I'm good at having sex—'"

"I'm good at having sex!"

"'I'm a slut for cock.'"

"I'm a—I'm a—"

He stroked her again, the lightest teasing touch. She twisted her hips as he withdrew his finger, aching to feel the pleasure again.

"Say it."

"I'm a s-slut for cock."

"Like you mean it." He held her hips still and leaned over her to pull a taut nipple into his mouth. He nipped at it with his rough lips, then bit down on it.

"Oh God!" she cried. "I'm a slut for cock!"

"Yes, you are." He licked the beating pulse in her neck. "And you're going to come for me like the sex-starved, cock-loving slut that you are. Do you understand me?"

"Yes, Sir!"

He put his hands on his thick length, stroking it before her eyes.

"If I give you my cock, you better let me know how much you like it."

"Yes, yes, please—I will—" She watched as he reached for a drawer in the side table. He pulled out a condom and ripped open the package. The five seconds he took to put it on seemed an eternity. She wasn't able to move more than a few inches in any direction. She felt helpless and trapped, which only made her pussy ache harder.

He gentled her with a hand on her shoulder, a firm kiss on her hair. She steeled herself not to shift, not to fidget. He hadn't told her specifically not to, but she was pretty sure by now what was expected of her at times like this: pure, still obedience. The concession that she was his. That every sound, every movement, every gasp or sigh was to be the result of his own hand. His palm stroked down to rest on her pubic bone. She shivered as he aligned himself even more closely to her. Now truly they would be joined in every manner of the word.

Please. Sex.

She felt the unforgiving steel of his muscles press against her front, felt him positioning his cock at her entrance.

Please...I don't care what our relationship is. I don't care.

I don't care if I get in trouble; I don't care if everyone knows.

I don't even care if you hurt me.

Please. Please. Have sex with me now.

She trembled in helpless anticipation as he took hold of her hips and slowly pushed inside. Oh God. How long had she needed to be filled like this? She gasped, amazed at the depth of sensation, amazed at how perfectly he fit. She arched her hips toward him, wanting more. He held her down as she tugged at the ropes.

"Okay. I've got you."

Her entire body was alive and humming with arousal. She'd never in her life felt this kind of pleasure before. He slid out and then in again, moving over her like waves in the ocean, forward, back, sweeping her up in his pull. He bent his head, kissed and licked her neck, then closed his teeth on the skin beneath her ear. She cried out, and his answering growl rumbled against her cheek. He pressed against her and entered her even more deeply; she felt the strange sensation of being one creature with him.

"Jackson!" She pulled hard at the ropes, needing to touch him. Needing to pull him closer, needing to push him away. He shuddered and went still in her. She felt his hot breath in her hair as she tossed her head back and forth.

"I know, baby," he said. He slowly drove in again. "I know."

"Please!"

She felt so aroused, so overstimulated, the throbbing almost felt like pain. She needed release. She moaned and arched against him. "Please! Please!"

"Shhh." He rocked in her, brushing back her hair. His cock, the ropes, all of it held her captured. "I've got you, little Prosperity," he whispered against her ear. "I've got you tied down tight."

He pushed into her again, lifting her hips from the bed. Her whole body tensed, hovering on the edge. Her mind turned off, and she felt only him, only fullness and sensation. Then she felt something inside her let go. She gasped from the force of the orgasm that seized her, pulling at the bonds that held her down. She bucked against Jackson, a wail bursting from her throat as the sensation peaked. Wave after wave of blissful, pleasurable ripples ran from her center to her trembling arms and her trapped legs.

"Jackson!" she cried. "Oh, Jackson. Oh God—"

He squeezed her, his head buried in her neck. His teeth opened against her skin and closed in a bite. She was still shuddering with aftershocks of pleasure as he groaned against her temple and found his own release.

Jackson lay next to her, gasping. So much for her not being very good at sex. He'd had to hold her down so she didn't injure them both, even restrained as she was. She'd been so small and tight, every stroke took him to heaven. He'd felt her in every single nerve, and by the time he'd come, he was wild for her like an animal. He was pretty sure he'd bitten her in the throes of his orgasm.

He looked over at her, exhausted beside him. Yes, a few teeth marks at the base of her neck, but no blood. There might be a light bruise. He usually had better control. He leaned down and traced the marked skin with the tip of his tongue. Her eyes fluttered, then closed again. Her frantic struggling of the moment before seemed to have given way to catatonia. He ran a light hand up her stockings.

"Okay?"

Her eyes opened and fixed on him. They were wet, intense.

"I... Wow... That was..."

"I know." He shifted to discard the condom, then turned back and began to stroke her with a light, feathery touch. He stroked over silk thighs, feminine hips, over her flat tummy that still rose and fell in long, irregular breaths. He considered whether or not to untie her. He would be hard again in five minutes, but Prosper looked spent. In fact, she appeared to be falling asleep.

"Hey." He pinched her cheek and leaned over to kiss her, thrusting his tongue deep inside her mouth, enjoying her sweet, sleepy reactions. "Wake up, girl. I need you again."

"No. Too tired."

"I think it wouldn't be very difficult for me to turn that no to a yes." He tweaked a nipple and laughed at its immediate response. "Not with you, anyway."

Her eyes opened again. She smiled, a tired smile, and laughed. A giddy laugh. They laughed together, then sobered.

"That was just…wow," she said. "I don't really have the words."

"I know. It was nice. You seemed to really enjoy it. I certainly did." He drank in her satisfied smile and then fingered the ropes around her slender wrists. *His.*

When he let her go, when he untied her and ushered her out of his apartment, she wouldn't be his anymore. Well, it had to be that way. But she would be his for a while, until he had to leave New York. They'd talk about that later.

For now, before he released her, he needed her again.

8 CHAPTER EIGHT

Prosper was supposed to be packing, but it was difficult to concentrate, especially with Glenna chattering in her ear.

"Tell me more about this date last night! It must have been something."

Prosper smiled. "It was great. He's really incredible."

"So who is this guy? Why don't you bring him along next time we all meet up for dinner?"

"I don't know. It's not really going anywhere."

"How do you know?"

"It's um...mostly physical."

"Mmm," said Glenna with a smirk. "It's like that, is it? Just using him? Hooking up? I didn't think you had it in you."

Prosper didn't think she had it in her either, but she'd actually set up a schedule to see Jackson on a regular basis for sex. Not just sex but all the other thrilling things. The *yes, Sirs* and *no, Sirs*, the rules and requirements. The punishments. It was all sex to her. She felt it all in the same hot, wet place.

Jackson had tied her to his bed and turned her entire world upside down. By the time he'd untied her, he'd had to pretty much dress her spent body and carry her downstairs to the cab he'd called. She would have given her entire fortune—which was not very much, admittedly—just to be allowed to sleep beside him all night, but no. Before he closed the door to the cab, he'd kissed her and said in her ear, "Friday. Same time. And absolutely no touching what's mine."

It had been easy last night, not touching, as she'd fallen, half-asleep already, into bed. But she woke up with quite the arousing collection of memories. She'd barely functioned all day. She'd flubbed and tripped so badly through rehearsals that Blake had snapped at her to concentrate. Jackson, however, was unusually patient, accepting her errors with a secret smirk on his face. Now she needed to pull herself together enough to pack up her things to move into her new apartment tomorrow, a tiny sublet a couple of blocks away.

"I'm so sorry you have to go," said Glenna, tucking some shoes and scarves into the box she packed. "I hope your new apartment works out."

"It's not exactly a showplace, but it'll do. Still, I can't believe I took a second job to afford an apartment that's barely large enough to hula-hoop in."

Glenna laughed. "Do you hula-hoop often? But I know what you're saying. Sometimes I think it would be better to just pack up and move home."

"Yeah, I think that too sometimes. But I don't even have that option, not really." Prosper wasn't on good terms with her mother or stepfather, and they were the only family she had. Her mother's family, of course, didn't even acknowledge that she existed. Her stepfather's family, while not under religious obligation to shun her, still felt pretty much the same.

She avoided Glenna's questioning gaze, turning away to search for the packing tape. The new apartment was a third-floor walk-up. She dreaded the idea of lugging her boxes up all those stairs even though she didn't have much. She considered calling Jackson for help. But that was something you did when someone was your boyfriend, wasn't it? Or your friend? As much as she hated to admit it, Jackson was neither. He was something very provocative, but a friend...no.

Friday night she arrived at Jackson's place still sore and achy from moving. She'd been stiff in rehearsals, but she'd explained the reason why, and he had gone easy on her, concentrating on the dancing princesses and their synchronization issues. Somehow she doubted he'd be as easygoing on her now. In fact, he led her straight to the bedroom.

"Undress and kneel," he ordered, pointing to a spot in the middle of the floor. "Take off everything. I want you naked as the day you were born."

She undressed and placed her clothes in a neat pile next to the door, then dropped to her knees where he'd pointed and sat back on her heels. She didn't know what was worse, the unaccustomed ache in her thighs or the nakedness. Not that a sheer bra or panties offered much more than a psychological feeling of being clothed.

He undressed too, then crossed to her and grabbed a handful of hair—not hard, but hard enough—and tugged her upward. "Kneel up. Legs slightly parted. Back straight. How's the new apartment?"

"The new apartment... It's okay, Sir." She tried to kneel straight, ignoring the protest of her thighs.

"Just okay?"

She shifted. Now he wanted to talk? Her scalp stung, her legs and hips were sore, and her mind was on other things, like the insistent erection rising before her eyes. And what to say about the apartment? It was small, dark, and in dire need of pest control. "It's a place to live, I guess."

"That bad?"

She shrugged, then yelped as his hand cracked across her ass. Proper address.

"Yes, Sir! It's bad! But it's okay."

He watched her shift again, then cocked his head to the side. "You really are sore, aren't you? Come here."

He helped her up, then knelt and ran firm fingers down the front of both her thighs to just above her knees. "Here?"

"Yes, Sir. But I can manage—"

"Lie down." He guided her to the bed. She tensed as he pushed her back and crawled between her legs.

"Relax, girl." He sat back and took her left leg in his hands, and started to rub it. "I'm just going to massage your leg. This will take some of the ache away."

There's only one thing that can take this ache away, she thought, staring up at him. His brows furrowed in concentration as he manipulated her muscles. She let her gaze travel lower to take in his half-erect cock. She remembered the feeling of it in her mouth, in her pussy, filling her up.

"Why didn't you call me?" Jackson's words drew her back from her salacious dreams. She opened her mouth and closed it, not sure what to say. "I could have helped you. Next time let me know." He picked up the other leg and worked the same magic. "I don't like when you're hurt. I don't want you wearing and tearing your body."

I want you to hurt me. I want you to wear me and tear me.

It was unbearable. If it were anyone else, she would have launched herself into his arms ten minutes ago, wrapped her legs tight around his hips, pressed her lips to his, lowered herself onto his cock—

What kind of slut was she turning into? She pursed her lips, trying not to think about how the heat from his fingertips radiated all the way to her pussy.

"You need to take care of these legs for me." He looked down at them, manipulated and caressed them, from the top of her thigh to the arch of her foot. "Point." She did, and he licked from the inside of her knee all the way up her leg. As he neared her center, she made an urgent sound. If he went any farther, she would lose control and thrust her pussy right up to his mouth.

He smiled. She was quite sure that he understood every impulse she felt. "Has anyone ever gone down on you?" His lips kissed ever closer to the part of her that felt like it was going to explode.

"N-no, Sir."

"Why not? They didn't offer, or you didn't want it?"

"I didn't want it." She told him the truth even though she knew she'd get a disapproving look.

"Didn't you think it would feel good?" His tongue, warm and wet, lapped once, twice across her center. She gasped. Her clit was so swollen, so sensitive. He licked her again, harder. The throb became a resonating urge.

"Please!" She reached down to grasp at his shoulders. He made a sharp noise and took her hands in his. He pinned them to the bed and glared down at her.

"Please, what?"

"Please, Sir, please—" She clenched her teeth as he nipped at her clit, then licked at the gorgeous ache he left behind.

"Ask me, if you want it. I'll make you come this way if you ask nicely."

"I can't!" She'd never be able to reach orgasm like this. It was too intimate, the way he was licking her, exploring her with his lips, his mouth. God, he was... God! How did his tongue get there?

"I can't come like this, Sir! Please, I just know I can't—"

Jackson laughed. "I give it a minute and a half." *No, no...* But oh God, it felt good. Soon the doubt in her mind was replaced by an ache in her pelvis that prevented any kind of logical thought. Any embarrassment and shame she felt was replaced by wonder at the things his tongue was making her feel and the desire for him to never stop. She came close, closer. She pulled at his hands where he held her, but he didn't let go. He sucked on her clit, then licked it in rhythmic strokes that made her hips jerk.

"Oh God! God! Please! Please, I'm going to come, Sir!"

He made a sound of assent, and she howled, her hands trapped in his fists. Her walls contracted, and her whole body tensed. Her world was reduced to his hot breath on her clit and the glorious pleasure that washed over her body. The orgasms he gave her seemed multicolored and multilayered compared to the ones she'd had before.

He held her down, and she reveled in his control until the last shudder left her and her breathing calmed.

"Thank you, Sir," he prompted when she could speak again.

"Thank you, Sir," she said with such avid gratefulness that Jackson chuckled against her inner thigh. He knelt up again between her legs. The magical mouth that had made her lose her mind now frowned as he studied her body.

"Is that one of mine?" he asked, pointing to a bruise on her calf.

"No, Sir. One of Blake's. The crossover to the *rond de jambe.*"

"Clod," he muttered under his breath. "What about here? Do you hurt here?" He began to massage her hip with agile fingers. "Your extension was terrible today."

"Yes, Sir. It does hurt. I'm sorry about my extension—"

He leaned down and closed his lips over hers. She reached for his neck, wound tentative fingers in his short, disheveled hair. She marveled at how soft it was. He didn't tell her to stop, so she pulled him closer. His breath tickled her brow and blew down her neck. He kissed her, endless kisses, fast, slow, wet, deep. His fingers on her hip didn't stop, not once. They continued to knead the ache away as he fed on her lips, sucked on her tongue. He captured her tiny moans and pleas in his mouth that still tasted faintly of her.

Her desire had only been whetted by the orgasm he gave her. She wanted to feel him inside her, feel him overpower her with his strength and his cock. But he seemed to enjoy teasing her in her needy condition. He cupped her face, licked her lips, made soothing sounds that only fueled the flames. She gazed up at him with a soft whine.

"Prosper," he whispered against her ear. "What's the matter?"

"Please, Sir! Please!"

Oh, the begging was gorgeous. He almost came right there, right on her belly, as he knelt over her. She begged so well, not fake like so many women. It was breathless, primitive begging. He thought he was probably falling in love.

He turned her over and parted her thighs wide with his knees. He stretched her arms high above her head and held them against the sheets. Her gorgeous ass arched off the bed, round and inviting. He wanted to spank it, make it scarlet and sore, but he couldn't take the time for that now. Any hunger she felt, he was sure he felt tenfold. "I'm going to fuck you," he said. "You lie there and wait."

He got up, rolled on a condom. When he knelt back on the bed, he pulled her hips up and held them firmly in his hands. It was good that he'd made her come earlier because he wouldn't last long enough to make her come again. He pulled her arms back down and made her cross her wrists at the small of her back. He held them there with one hand, while his other hand snaked around the front of her to hold her fast for his initial deep thrust.

She cried out, a sexy sound that drove him crazy. She was so alive, so responsive when he fucked her, he could practically feel her nerves vibrating against his skin. How could she be so serious and reserved in the studio and yet so unfettered in bed? It confounded him. But he couldn't think of that now. He wanted to think about fucking her, plunging his cock inside her again and again as he held her so she couldn't get away. He looked down and watched his length slide in and out of her pussy, advancing and retreating. He slammed his pelvis against her lovely cheeks, still holding her restrained. He basked in the feeling of controlling and possessing something so wild. His captured creature.

He wanted to fuck her forever, hold her down until his strength gave out, but soon enough he was losing control. One particularly throaty moan and snap of her hips pushed him over the edge. His groin and balls tightened almost painfully, and he came in a white heat. He held her wrists hard as he rode out the throb and release of orgasm inside her hot channel. He didn't let her arms go until his dick had emptied itself completely.

He held her still, just kneeling over her, looking down at her prone figure. He had pushed her shoulders down on the bed so her back was arched. It rose and fell with each soft breath. If she had expected him to make her come, she didn't make any remarks or pout about it. Good sub. She would come when he wanted her to come.

He noted with satisfaction that she was completely calm and relaxed now. His cock-tamed slut. He rubbed the small of her back as he pulled out and tossed the condom in the bedside trash.

"All better?"

"Yes, Sir. Thank you." Her soft voice trembled with raw emotion.

"No, don't get riled up." He grabbed a fistful of hair and nuzzled his face into her nape. "Are you mine? Yes or no?"

"Yes, Sir."

"Yes, you are mine. I'll take care of you for as long as you belong to me. Do you know that, girl?"

"I... Thank you, Sir...so much."

"Come here."

He pulled her back against him and wrapped his arms around her. He held her close between his knees.

"Are your legs still sore?"

"No, Sir. Not very much."

"You have a beautiful body. And it pleased me very much, the way you gave yourself to me today. Do you understand what I mean?"

"I—I think so. Yes, Sir."

"I like for you to be completely open to me. Mine to take. I don't want you thinking about your own pleasure except as it pleases me. I like you to serve me in that way."

She sniffled and turned her head to rest it against his chest. "That's what I want. I just want to serve you."

"That's what makes you happy, yes? Making me happy?"

"Yes, Sir."

"And that's why I don't want you touching yourself when I'm not around. Have you been keeping your hands to yourself?"

"Mmm...so far I've managed it."

He laughed at that, and pulled her closer so they were skin to flushed skin.

"Try to be perfect for me. Yes, Prosper? Obey my rules. Or I'll punish you."

She shivered a little.

"What is it?"

"Will you...will you only punish me when I've broken a rule?"

Damn if she didn't sound disappointed. He turned her face up to his.

"Do you want to be punished at other times? Have I got a little masochist on my hands?"

"No. I don't know. I don't know what I want. And it doesn't matter anyway...does it?"

Jackson thought a long moment. It didn't matter, since he was the one in charge, but his curiosity was piqued.

"I reward for good behavior, just as I punish for bad. Tell me what you want, girl. If you're honest and truthful, you might get it."

He turned her and laid her back on the bed, then leaned over her. He looked into her eyes. He could see the internal struggle there. Embarrassment, excitement. Shyness and desire. He thought for a moment of the irony of training assertiveness into a submissive. But he was a great believer in the "campsite rule," leaving your subs in better condition than they were when you arrived. *Talk, Prosper. Ask for what you want.*

"I...I..."

"Louder."

Her eyes darted past his shoulder, and she took a deep breath. "I had this...thing I was thinking about—"

"Look at me. Look in my eyes and talk. Do it right, or you won't get what you want."

A ferocious flush spread across her cheeks all the way to her ears. "It's embarrassing."

"I know it is, but tell me anyway. Look at me and talk."

"Okay. I had a fantasy of you," she began in a stronger voice. "It was before, before I knew you were..."

"A pervert?"

She giggled. "A dominant. Before I knew that any of this was ever going to happen in real life. It was a fantasy that you rolled your sleeves up and gave me this stern look and then pulled me over your lap."

"And what did I do then?" he asked.

"That's where the fantasy ended. I never let it get past that point."

"Why not?"

"I was too embarrassed. You were my boss."

"I'm still your boss, in every sense of the word."

"I was afraid you'd look at me and know it. What I was thinking."

He laughed. "Honestly, I had no idea." She smiled back at him, her blush subsiding at last. "Prosper, I want you to tell me—if you had let your fantasy continue, what I would have done to you?"

She thought a moment.

"I think I wanted you to do whatever you wanted to do to me. And I didn't know what that was, but whatever it was, I wanted to take it, for you."

His gut clenched with desire. "Good answer."

He stood without a word and started to dress. Pulled his pants over his thickening erection, pulled on his shirt, buttoned it up. Then he fixed her with a look.

"Stand up. Put your panties on." He threw them to her. She faced him, wringing her hands. He let her wait and worry over what was coming while he walked downstairs to the kitchen to get a chair and bring it back to the room. He put it down just inside the door with a sharp crack, then crossed to the bureau. He opened the bottom drawer and drew out a black leather paddle. He dropped it on the chair, thrilling to the wide-eyed look on Prosper's face. Then he reached for his right cuff, flicked his wrist, gave her the look, the look all submissives recognized. She bit her lip. He started rolling up the first sleeve with an exaggerated frown on his face.

He watched her shift, playing her part beautifully. Her distress was gorgeous and, well, probably partly real. He reached for the other sleeve, unbuttoned the cuff, flipped the sleeve up to his elbow. For extra effect he flexed his forearms, then picked up the leather paddle from the chair and stood up to his full height.

"Come here, Prosper. Now."

She took her time crossing to him. He noted as he seated himself in the wooden chair that her breath was already coming faster. He glared at her to heighten the fantasy, and she dropped her eyes like a naughty little girl.

Never mind that she hadn't been naughty. It didn't really matter. He took her arm and pulled her closer none too gently, then draped her over his knee. She was shivery. The paddle did look forbidding, but he wouldn't hurt her with it. Much. This was playtime, after all.

He pulled her panties down to just above her knees. She tensed as he caressed her trembling bare cheeks. He gave her some warm-up smacks, and she pressed her face into the side of his leg. When her bottom was nice and pink, he spanked harder. Almost immediately she started to struggle.

He made a warning sound and held her more firmly with his palm on the small of her back. More sharp spanks without any respite in between. *Smack. Smack. Smack.* The paddle made a spectacular sound even when he wasn't using it full force. He still hurt her, because he knew she needed it. When she started to squirm, he focused her again.

"Behave. None of this fidgeting around. This isn't even a hard spanking." Her indignant groan made him laugh. "Would you like me to hit you harder?" Her groan turned to a whine, and he pinched her inner thigh when she tried to grind against his leg. "Not yet. Soon." He landed a few more blows, but his mind was headed elsewhere, watching her squirming ass over his lap. He reached between her legs and slipped his fingers down to her opening. She was hot and dripping wet.

"Please!" she gasped.

He dropped the paddle and pushed her onto her back on the floor. He took his pants down to his knees and fell on her. Her squeak of alarm reminded him he needed a condom. He crawled to the nightstand and ripped open the drawer, then returned to her.

"Arms over your head." His voice came out sounding more like a growl than human speech. He pulled her panties off, then slapped her thighs open. She spread them wide, watching with big eyes as he rolled the condom on. He put his arms around her and gathered her hot, paddled ass in his hands. She arched her pelvis against him, and he slid inside her all the way to the hilt. His blood hissed in his ears from the intense sensation of being enveloped by her.

"My God, girl. The way you feel..."

He fucked her, cradling her close. Since he made her keep her arms over her head, her back was arched and her breasts were thrust forward. He took full advantage, licking and biting her exposed nipples. She squirmed under him, and her hips snapped against his. They were both uncontrolled, caught up in a frenzy of sexual pleasure. Some part of him was afraid of hurting her, but another part of him was powerless to stop driving in her with all his strength. When he felt her walls contract, felt her quake against him, he kissed her hard and caught her gasps in his mouth. Those gasps were already ingrained in his psyche, deeply familiar to him. Like an animal, he reacted in kind. He clutched her and rocked against her, let his own orgasm shake him free of the world. Gasp, sigh, shudder, melt into oblivion. He already knew her inside and out.

9 CHAPTER NINE

She slept in his bed, and he watched her. Their scene had been so long and involved that he hadn't felt comfortable letting her go home. Nor was he ready to crawl into bed beside her and sleep. Not yet.

He ran his eyes over every part of her for the hundredth time. She was naked—he'd insisted on that—and curled up in his bed like a kitten. A stray kitten that was grateful for a home.

He frowned. It was dangerous ground, this. To think about how lovely and natural she looked there in his bed, to think about the possibilities. A full-time D/s arrangement would be complicated, if not impossible. He couldn't be around her without wanting to control, to own. To grope and fuck. It wouldn't only drain him; it would drain her too. It would be too much on top of everything else. He didn't want her moving in. It would be bad for them both.

But he ought to take her in, his conscience chided. She was going to be waitressing after performances, for fuck's sake, to pay for her new place. After rehearsals and class and makeup and stage calls and curtain calls, she'd be trudging off to work. After dancing his *Firebird*, she would be fetching beers for frat boys and horny businessmen. It would be easy to put her up, a small, quiet girl like her.

No.

No, it wasn't fair to lead her on that way, to offer what could only be temporary help. Soon he'd be going back to Chicago. He already had work lined up, commitments.

He ran a finger up her calf. They fascinated him, her calves. So feminine and yet so strong even in repose, the shapely, lithe muscle tapering to the impossibly tiny ankle. Like those racehorses whose ankles looked ready at any moment to snap. He shook his head. No thoughts of snapping. If that clod Blake ever dropped her or caused her injury, Jackson would kill him. No, she was stronger than she looked, he knew.

She didn't need him. He intended to keep it that way. For her, not for him.

He crawled into bed with a sigh, pulled the covers over both of them. She was on the side he'd pointed to when he'd ordered her to stay the night. He'd intended to stay on his side but found her sleepy, sated body impossible to resist. He curled around her, fascinated as always by how petite she was. His hairy thighs dwarfed her smooth ones, and when she turned and nestled into his chest, her head fit perfectly under his chin. He ran his hand down her arm and rested it on her hip. Her skin looked like delicate porcelain under his tan, hirsute fingers. He smiled at how deeply she slept. She shifted closer to him but didn't wake. Sex seemed to unwind her. Hell, it tranquilized her.

And he had capitalized on the opportunity, pressed her to conversation as they lay on the floor afterward. She had been so relaxed and open to him. He'd asked her about her dancing, about what drove her. They talked about ballet companies—the New York City Ballet, the Joffrey, the Ballets Russes—and about Alvin Ailey and the way modern dance moved and thrilled her. But when he suggested she move to a modern dance company, she shook her head, the calm relaxation chased away and replaced with doubt about her capabilities.

Damn, the girl was capable as hell. He wished she were less hard on herself. He knew she would be happier if she were. He wished he could figure out the terror behind her eyes that she might disappoint, that she might fall short. That even her typical perfect would never be good enough.

Prosper looked up at the tattooed and pierced bartender as he loaded her tray with drinks. "Don't drop it, love," he said with a wink.

She didn't smile. It would be a miracle if she could thread her way across the club without dropping drinks again. She'd done it yesterday when an overexuberant patron had thrust his hand up her skirt and nearly insinuated his fingers into her panties. She'd dropped the beers on the head of an older man and his wife, who had drunkenly insisted she be fired. The manager had comped their tab for the night and taken it out of her tips, so she'd basically worked for free.

She picked back and forth, avoiding anyone who looked the least bit dicey, and finally arrived at the table to drop off the drinks without incident. The music pounded in her ears, and every pore of her being felt saturated with smoke. It was nearly one, and the place was still filling up. When would the bar start to thin out so she could walk through without brushing against body after body? She was still too aroused from her time with Jackson the other night.

Still aroused? She was constantly aroused. She didn't know how she made it through class anymore, constantly watching for Jackson to pass by in the hall outside the window. Then there was that moment when she arrived at rehearsal, when she had to settle herself so she didn't go in and fall at his feet. The looks he gave her made her wish they were still rehearsing alone instead of with the whole cast.

Crap. She was headed for a new table and realized too late the faces she knew. Blake, Kristen, Elsa, Ed. There was no time to turn, to make her way back through the crowded press of people that had already closed behind her. And the table was in her section, so she had to go wait on them. She stalked up to the group of dancers with a frown. Kristen smirked and narrowed her eyes. Elsa ignored her, and Ed seemed to not even realize who she was.

"Prosper! What are you doing here?" yelled Blake.

"I told you yesterday I was working here."

He shrugged and gestured over his shoulder. "I saw Jackson back there."

"What?"

"He's here. I saw him when we came in."

She resisted the urge to look around, to see if Jackson was really there. He would have told her if he was coming. Wouldn't he? The dancers placed their orders, and Prosper somehow restrained herself from rolling her eyes at Kristen's tone. She hated that she was working while they were able to relax and have fun. Every moment she fought the impulse to quit, to sling her tray across the club and take off Kristen's head with it, storm out and curse them all to hell. And Blake must be mistaken. Jackson couldn't be here, or she would know. If he was anywhere in her vicinity, she would know at once, feel it in every bone and muscle.

She stole a look around the room anyway. In the darkness, the pounding mass of bodies, it was impossible to tell if one very tall and very sexy blond-haired, blue-eyed choreographer was watching her from some alcove across the bar. If he was here, was it to see her? Or might he have come to find someone else to take home? She was with him just a couple of nights a week by agreement. She had no idea what he did the other five nights and no right to complain if there were five other girls, one for each day. What did she really know about him? Nothing. That he was talented, demanding, handsome, sexy. The kind of man who probably didn't need to be alone if he didn't want to be.

She headed back to the bar. She hoped he wasn't there. She didn't want him to see her like this, tripping across a crowded bar, getting smoke blown in her face, getting felt up, spilling untold amounts of beer on her clothes, on her dress. So much for the graceful Firebird.

She went up on her toes and bent over to yell the order to the bartender—all those piercings!—and slapped at the uninvited hand that groped up her dress. "Do you mind?" she yelled at the offender, a middle-aged businessman with sweat rings on his shirt. Ugh. What was she doing here, getting felt up by gross men while she waited for drinks to take to a table of people she hated?

When her shift was finally up, it was almost three. She wanted to climb into bed. She blew money on a cab because the night before someone had trailed her home at a distance and scared her half to death. At her building she trudged up the three flights of stairs, motivated by thoughts of a hot, cleansing shower, only to find the hot water was gone. She showered anyway, shivering, needing to wash off the smoke and alcohol. The noise of the water almost, but not quite, drowned out the loud sex taking place next door.

By the time the arguing started in the apartment on the other side, Prosper was desperate for sleep. She pulled her pillow over her head and squeezed her eyes shut.

Jackson tossed in bed, unable to stop thinking about Prosper. He hated that she worked at Halo, and he hated that he stalked her there like some kind of socially maladjusted idiot. He'd skulked at a table in the far corner of the dark nightclub as soon as he knew for sure that Prosper wasn't working in that area. He'd nursed a couple of beers and fended off a parade of rather persistent women. All he really accomplished was a dull buzz and a fit of guilt that he wasn't dragging her out of there and insisting she quit.

But he had no right to do that, not unless he was going to find her another place to work, another source of income. Holy fuck, why was New York so expensive? Why were dancers not paid enough to find a place to live?

You have a place she could live.

Fucking conscience. But it wasn't fair to provide her a place to live and then throw her back on the streets in a few weeks, back where she'd started. *But in the meantime, she could be saving rent for later.*

He flipped over with an angry grunt. Why did it all bother him so much? Prosper held her own against the rude patrons, but it was hard for him not to get involved. Jackson wanted to rip their arms off and make them apologize to her from under his boot on the floor. But no, he didn't do that. He fled. He stormed out of the bar before he made a scene he would regret. Before he made such a scene that Prosper would notice him there. He didn't want her to know he followed her around. He didn't want her to know he had followed her home last night to be sure she arrived safely. He didn't want her to know he thought about her almost all the time.

Monday morning he waited with Blake for Prosper. Late again. Hiding out somewhere, since she no longer fit in anywhere. His fault.

"I saw you at Halo," said Blake when the silence became untenable. "At least I thought I did."

"Halo?" *Shit.* All his skulking around was for nothing if Blake ratted him out to Prosper. He decided to play it off. "I might have dropped in. I've been checking out some of the local bars."

He could tell Blake wasn't convinced by his indifferent act. "Prosper works there, you know."

"Does she? I don't much care as long as she's where I need her to be when I need her. Speaking of which"—Jackson crossed to the door to look down the hall—"was she in class?"

"Yeah. I saw Kristen talking to her afterward."

Jackson's jaw tightened. He'd seen Kristen "talk" to her more than once. He didn't want to get involved. Petty dancer feuds weren't his business, but the whole situation pissed him off. "Why don't you call off your friends?"

Blake laughed. "As if I have the power to do that."

"You're with her, aren't you? Kristen?"

"Sometimes. But there's nothing I can do about what she does. The way she is. And Prosper took the role Kristen wanted."

"She didn't take it. I gave it to her. Anyway, Kristen couldn't do the role, not the way I want it. Why don't you tell her that?"

"Why don't you tell her?"

The men faced off just as Prosper arrived, trying overly hard to be breezy and casual. "Sorry I'm late."

He didn't have to look in her eyes to know she was upset. He knew her well enough by now. He shot Blake a meaningful glare, which Blake ignored. Suddenly Jackson didn't want Blake to touch her at all. He ran Prosper through the opening combination himself instead, refining and perfecting steps while Blake leaned against the wall with a scowl. Jackson was always spellbound when he partnered her. Her body was so strong. She was fully invested in the steps, and her lines were striking, perfect. She demonstrated amazing control.

So unlike the Prosper who came to him at night. *Tonight.* It was Wednesday. She would come to him tonight. He looked forward to her visits with such intensity; he lived in fear that she would cancel, that she might not to show up. He stopped, looked in her eyes as she balanced through a slow *rond de jambe.*

Yes, she would come.

He gestured Blake over and retreated behind the piano. He directed the pair from there, through the complicated opening pas de deux. The teasing, the flirting, the passion. The capture, and then the release.

10 CHAPTER TEN

Before she even arrived at Jackson's house, Prosper was beside herself with excitement. She rang the bell and waited with her legs pressed together and her arms crossed over her chest. It was freezing. He'd offered to come to her place, but Prosper had no desire to spend any more time there than she had to.

She heard the lock turn, and there he was. Scary blue eyes, weed-whacker hair, and that smile... Jackson pulled her in the door and crushed her to his chest. She felt all the tension and anxiety of the day fade away. His rough lips covered hers. His mouth captured her moans, and sparks shot to her breasts and down into her pelvis. He reached under her dress, felt the stockings. He snapped a garter against the back of her thigh, which made her jump; then he dipped his fingers between her legs. She held on to his shoulders, made a noise as he probed her so deeply she had to rise up on her toes. Same intimate greeting every time. She lived for it.

He drew away, and his hands went to his belt. "Did you touch yourself since I saw you last?"

"No, Sir." She shrank back as he pulled it off and clutched her hands together. "I wanted to...but I—I didn't."

He scrutinized her as if gauging her truthfulness. Then he doubled the belt over and pointed to a spot on the floor.

"Kneel. Bend over. Forehead on the floor."

Her mouth fell open. She'd told the truth, and he was going to punish her anyway. "Please, I didn't—" At a sharp crack of the belt on the floor, she scooted forward. She knelt and braced herself as he pulled up her skirt. It was so unfair!

She made fists next to her face when the first blow fell. She was terrified that soon she'd have to use them to shield herself, to push herself up from the floor and run away. Two, three, four, each harder than the last. She didn't know what was more painful, the bite of the leather on her flesh or the fact that she was being punished for no reason at all. She supposed there was a reason—he wanted her to take it. But each new blow had her doubting her ability to please him, doubting her ability to take the pain. His belt fell hard against her ass, impact that grew and bloomed into a raw, burning sensation. She whined against the floor, taking deep breaths to steady herself. The strokes fell on top of one another, building to an impossible level of stinging torment. She shifted away from him, collapsing on her side, automatic self-preservation. His displeased grunt barely registered through the panic in her brain, the fire in her ass cheeks. He tapped her hip with the belt.

"Up."

His voice was low and stern, a provocative rumble that made her shudder. She righted herself, put her ass back in the air, and braced for more pain. He was trying to hurt her, and that thought both aroused and scared her. Five, six, seven, eight! She tensed between blows, waiting for the next one in dread. She wanted to pull away each time, shrink away from the cruel torment, but she didn't want to fail him. How many would he give her? Her ass throbbed, and she cried out into the carpet at each fresh explosion of pain. When she was a tense, quivering mess and was sure she couldn't endure one more, she heard the belt drop on the floor.

He knelt beside her and ran his hand up her back.

"Okay," he said in that voice that really did make everything seem okay, even when everything really wasn't. His rough, warm hand caressed her cheek and then clamped over her mouth. He knelt behind her and leaned over her back, enveloping contact that calmed and excited her at the same time. He left her a moment to push his pants off and put on a condom. Her breath rasped heavy and frantic, like an animal pursued. Maybe that's what she was.

He put his hand back over her mouth as he returned and drove inside. She reached back for him, needing the contact. Needing to know he wouldn't let her go.

"I've got you," he said against her ear, his soothing voice a bizarre contrast to his violent thrusts. "Keep your hands right there on the floor." He fucked her roughly, and his hand over her mouth aroused her as much as the cock between her legs. She felt forced and possessed in a primal way. With each thrust he contacted her sore ass, her aching cheeks. She began to pant. The hot pleasure at her core spread, growing and unfolding. She wanted to touch herself. She needed release.

"Do you want to come, Prosper?"

She moaned behind his hand. How could she possibly form words? She tried to focus, she tried to think, but her entire world was the throb and jolt of his cock filling her. Yes, she wanted to come, yes! She nodded, arching her back.

He reached beneath her and pinched her clit, then massaged it with his fingers. She shivered under him, overwhelmed by the sensation of tingly pressure in her pussy that spread through her entire pelvis. His rough fingers conjured hot pleasure so it seemed to slide all around her body, making her wiggle and arch for more. He slapped her sensitive nub once, twice, then stroked it with a dexterity that made the whine in her throat rise to a cry and made her hips buck wildly.

"Yes, I know," he said. "I know it feels good." The pounding never stopped. It drove her; it held her. It pummeled her into a frighteningly submissive space. At the same time his fingertips played over her clit, made her writhe and squirm and, finally, cry out in an attenuated wail against his palm.

"Come for me, girl. I want to feel it."

The intensity reached a peak she could hardly bear, and she let go. Everything swirled together in one great jumble of hectic pleasure: his thick cock, the slap of his hips against her sore ass, the immovability of his hand over her mouth, the tortured cry she released behind its grasp. The force he'd created inside her, all over her, broke wide in a shimmering orgasm that possessed every part of her: lips, breasts, nipples, knees, even her toes, which curled with the intensity of the release. She felt a warm, shuddering ebb of tension that left her limp and satiated.

Then he gathered her close as his hand left her mouth and twisted in her hair. He thrust in her right to the hilt, clutching her so tightly he squeezed the air right out of her. She gasped and gave her body up to his power, to his hard, animalistic fucking, to the scratch of his chest hair on her back, the taut muscles of his abdomen pressing her down. His cock was the fulcrum that held her and defined her, and she wanted nothing more at that moment than to be defined by him. She felt owned, possessed, each shallow breath drawn only as far into her lungs as he allowed. When he finally grew still, when his shudders subsided, only then did his arm loosen enough to let her take a deep breath. His fist in her hair unfurled, his fingers weaving themselves through her locks down to her nape. He squeezed the back of her neck, and she sighed from the pleasure of it.

He pulled away. He slapped her sore cheeks and pulled her up so her head fell back against his chest. He held her there, reached around, and pinched first one nipple, then the other. She was still painfully sensitive from the orgasm. She made some plaintive sounds, but he only pinched them both harder and held them until she settled into the pain.

"Good girl. I do what I want to you, don't I?"

"Yes, Sir."

He nuzzled her, breathing down the curve of her shoulder. "I hurt you even when you haven't been bad. Then I fuck you like a little slut, and the harder I fuck you, the harder you come. Isn't that true?"

What other answer was there? "Yes, Sir."

"'Yes, Sir. I love to be hurt and then fucked like a slut.'"

She repeated it nice and loud, the way he liked.

"Get dressed," he said when he finally released her. "We're going out."

He sat across from her and stared, his face set like stone. She looked back, looked down, looked around the darkened restaurant, a small, authentic Chinese place. Tinkling ethnic music came over the speakers. Prosper didn't know if it was actually erotic or only sounded erotic because of the way she felt. She took a deep breath and tried to calm the agitation surging in a part of her body that felt like her heart. Not her real heart, but that cartoon heart that pounded a foot out of the character's chest when they fell in love, two curved arches tapering down to one point.

"So." Jackson leaned back and looked away from her. She couldn't read his expression. She didn't know him that well, not yet. And he wasn't one of those men who wore his emotions on his sleeve. "So," he said again, turning back to her.

She wrung her hands under the table. "Are we still playing?"

"I don't know. You tell me."

"This doesn't feel like a game anymore."

"No, it doesn't. Not to me either."

She ducked her head as the waitress came. Jackson ordered for both of them, tempura and mu shu with Chinese wine. When she left with the menus, he rubbed his face and leaned on the table.

"Listen, I have to be honest with you. I'm only here until we mount the ballet. That won't change. It can't. I have too many important things lined up back home."

She nodded, then caught herself, whispered, "Yes, Sir," and wondered if she'd ever be normal again. If she'd ever be able to nod her head or shake a negative without hearing his sharp *answer me* fire in her brain.

"You work in a company here. Most of the great companies are here, so this is a great place for you to be. Look, I just think we need to be real here. This can only go so far."

Prosper nodded. "I know. Sure."

"Unless..." He paused, then fell silent. "I don't know."

She needed him to guide her. She needed him to tell her the next steps, and she would do them. But he said nothing more for a long time. He left her with her thoughts and with a terrible fear of saying the wrong thing. She was so afraid of saying the wrong thing that she said nothing at all. They sat there together, silent, until the cheerful waitress reappeared with the food. Prosper watched him smile at the server, help her arrange the dishes on the table. *No strings attached.* No matter how he made her feel, they had gone into this with an agreement.

He began to eat, but she had no appetite. She pretended to eat, pushing her food around on her plate. Jackson took a sip of wine and then leaned forward to look at her with that same inscrutable look on his face.

"When I dance with you, it feels different than anyone I've ever danced with before," he said. "Why do you think that is?"

"I don't know. But I feel the same way. You make me feel..." Her voice trailed off. She was going to say something stupid.

"Feel what? Tell me."

"I don't know. I only know that I'm scared to be with you and I'm scared not to be with you."

He was quiet a long time. Then he drained the rest of his wine and said, "Yeah. Me too."

He turned the topic to safer things: company politics, upcoming ballets, details about the Firebird costume she'd been fitted for earlier in the week. Later, he didn't take her back to his home again, although he insisted on walking her up all three flights to her door. She reassured him that the screams and thumps coming from the apartment next door were nothing unusual. She couldn't help thinking of Jackson's neat, quiet house.

Big bed, clean sheets, Jackson right there every night. But she reminded herself it wouldn't work out anyway, living with Jackson. He would see her as she really was: neurotic, imperfect. He'd see her with her morning bedhead and see her rubbing her aching feet every night. See her waxing, plucking her brows, flossing. She imagined them standing side by side brushing their teeth. Oh Lord, no.

"Sunday night, then?" he asked as the yelling from the neighboring apartment reached a fever pitch.

"Yeah. That sounds good."

He rubbed his mouth, then pulled her close, gave her ass one last squeeze. "I'll see you at rehearsal."

"Sure. Yes. Okay."

He kissed her and then fixed her with a familiar, stern look, leaning in close to breathe down her neck.

"No touching what's mine, girl. Don't dare."

"No, Sir," she whispered next to his ear. "I won't."

She was graceful, irresistible, even in the smoky bar, even trying to balance a tray while being jostled and groped by strangers. She was beautiful no matter what. He had yet to look at her and not feel drawn to her side. But no, he wouldn't go to her side like he wanted to. He was hiding like a pussy, back in his usual corner, the corner she never waited on and couldn't see from her cluster of tables. But he could see her. He thought he could see her through a dead man's fog, if for no other reason than her Firebird hair. He could smell her out of a mob scene. He would breathe her right into his body if there was a way.

Jackson thought again of how to proceed. Their meetings were more incendiary each time, the partings more excruciating. The veneer of impersonality, the strict, finite roles and interaction more and more impossible to bear. He thought about asking her to move in with him for the hundredth time. He even thought of which contacts in Chicago might have a place for Prosper to dance. Then he thought about how moving in together was always the beginning of the end.

But Jesus, the girl was dragging, tired from late nights. He'd actually talked her out of taking on extra nights at the bar and told her to give up either Friday or Saturday night, but she'd refused. He wished he could forbid her outright to work. He wished he had the right to control every part of her life. He would take much better care of her than she took of herself.

He could do it if he wanted. He could take more control of her. He could ask her to move in, ask her to consider a more encompassing D/s relationship. Not 24-7, but something more than the two short evenings a week they had now, the evenings that flew by and always left him craving more. He was fairly certain she would say yes, that she wanted more too. But like any good submissive, she deferred to him in everything. And he, for some inexplicable reason, was choosing to drag his feet.

He waved off the waitress when she came to his table. He didn't come here to drink. He looked past her to Prosper. Then Jackson noticed a rough-looking patron standing near the bar. The slimeball eyed Prosper up and down, flexed his arms in his muscle shirt. Jackson thought if one more guy groped her, he would lose his mind. But she moved by without incident. Then time stood still as Jackson watched the fight start.

From nowhere, from everywhere, it exploded. Bodies grappled; chairs knocked over. Fists and drinks flew through the air. Jackson catapulted off his stool and crossed the dark bar like a man possessed. Any bystander in his path was thrown out of the way. Somehow as the crowd re-formed around the combatants, Prosper became trapped in the line of the fight. He saw her bumped, saw her fly into the bar and crack the back of her head. She went down like a limp doll. He roared, and even the descending bouncers couldn't keep him away. He pushed and wove until he got to her and was confronted by another familiar face. Blake was lifting her from the floor, shielding her from the unruly crowd of bodies. When he looked from Blake back to her, all he could see was the blood.

Jackson stared while they put her on the backboard. God, there was so much blood. The cut wasn't large, but it was deep. It was the neck brace, though, that stole his breath away.

They carried her out through the kitchen, past the cop cars where the young men who'd been fighting were being pushed into backseats. Blake pulled Jackson past as if he knew the thoughts going through his mind.

"Let the cops take care of them. Prosper needs you. Come on."

In the cab on the way to the hospital, Jackson grilled Blake on what he'd seen of the fight.

"Did she hit her temple? How hard did she fall?"

"They'll do scans and stuff at the hospital, I'm sure. But uh, I actually heard her head hit the bar from where I was standing."

Jackson winced. He was thankful for a moment he hadn't been that close.

Blake's leg bounced in agitation. "I wish I could have helped her."

"I saw you. If you hadn't been there to help, she might have been trampled on top of everything else. Don't beat yourself up."

No, Jackson was doing enough of that himself. He should have forbidden her to work, should have taken her in. All the times he'd seen her groped and tripped and bumped and jostled, and he'd done nothing. All the bruises he saw on her when they scened that he knew weren't from him. And now she was in a neck brace on a backboard, bleeding like hellfire. All because of his selfish fear of getting involved.

At the hospital Jackson bit his nails while Blake leafed through magazines in the waiting room. After twenty minutes or so, Blake turned to him.

"I was right all along."

"Right about what?"

"You like her. You're going out with her. You're fucking, yeah?"

Jackson turned away. "Why do you say that?"

"Because you've just about bitten every fingernail off. And because you were at the bar."

"You were at the bar too."

"Yeah," he said. "Pointlessly, I guess."

Jackson's eyes narrowed. "You go there to see her? You have a thing for her?"

"Do you have a thing for her?" Blake shot back.

"She's dancing the lead in my ballet. I have a vested interest."

Blake snorted and sat back. "Vested interest. Is that what they're calling it now? It would look pretty bad if it got out."

"It's nobody's business."

"The secrecy is part of the fun, right? I mean, I suspected, but there was really no way to tell. I figured if you were going out, she wouldn't be working at that bar three nights a week and living in that roach-infested hole down from the theater."

Jackson tensed but pretended indifference. "I'm not real involved in her personal life."

Blake rolled his eyes. "Nice. Sport fuck your ballerina. Vested interest, my ass."

"Look, you don't understand." Jackson shut his mouth and turned away. It was none of Blake's business, and he certainly wouldn't appreciate the finer points of their relationship. *We have a Dom/sub arrangement, no strings attached. We meet two nights a week.*

The nurse came out, picked through the crowded waiting room to where Jackson and Blake sat.

"Excuse me. Are you the gentlemen who brought in Prosper Ware?"

Jackson was already on his feet.

"Yes—"

"Is she all right?" The men spoke at the same time.

"Yes, she'll be fine. The doctor will be happy to speak to anyone who's family. Are you family? Husband? Partner?"

"We're work acquaintances," Jackson said. He ignored Blake's snicker.

"I'm actually her partner," Blake said, but Jackson was already following the nurse toward the wide double doors.

"Her family isn't local, but she works for me. I'll be helping her home when she's discharged, so I'd love to speak to the doctor about what's going on."

Blake tagged along, undeterred by Jackson's irate glance. "Will she be able to leave tonight?"

"I don't think so," said the nurse. "We'll probably keep her overnight to be safe, but as far as serious damage—"

"Her neck? Her spine?" Jackson asked.

"All perfectly fine," the nurse reassured him as they neared Prosper's room. "She told me she was a dancer. I'm sure she'll dance again. She'll just need a few days of rest." She smiled at Jackson, but his gaze had already moved past her to the pale figure sleeping on the bed. His heart clenched to see how small and vulnerable she looked. She had a large white bandage wrapped around her head. He moved closer and was relieved to find her face relaxed. No tiny tension lines. Her chest rose and fell in a regular rhythm. He wanted nothing more on earth than to gather her close. She had to sleep though. He didn't want to wake her.

The doctor came by soon after, and Jackson caught most of the important details. CT scan results, aftercare for the stitches, seven good days of rest. He listened, but his mind was only half there.

"Can I stay?" he asked as soon as the doctor was finished. He didn't know why he posed it as a question, because he had no intention of leaving her side. Fortunately the doctor nodded.

Blake let out a long sigh. "I have class in—" He peered at his watch. "Ugh. Four hours. I've got to go. But I'm glad she's going to be okay."

Jackson extended his hand to Blake. "Thanks for your help. And about me and Prosper—"

"I won't tell anyone. For her sake. Not yours."

"I appreciate it."

With Blake gone, it was quiet. Jackson stared at Prosper in sleep. Her eyes were ringed by dark circles, and her face looked peaked. No, it wouldn't do. He wouldn't have her living this way. He settled beside her in a chair and waited for her to wake. It was time to say the things he needed to say.

11   CHAPTER ELEVEN

Prosper woke with a start in the darkened room. Weak light came from the gaps around the blinds and fell across the shaggy blond head next to her hand. Jackson.

He stirred, and she noticed then that her hand was in his, that he was gripping it tightly even in sleep. She stayed still, tried to remember the night before. She remembered the main details. The sudden fight, the painful fall. The faces all around her as she tried to stay awake but found the edge of her vision growing dim.

She remembered waking up in the hospital as they stitched her up. While they cleaned off the blood, a doctor showed her pictures of her brain and neck and told her everything was okay. But was she really okay? She did a quick inventory. Her legs moved with no soreness or stiffness. Her head was a little groggy, but she thought it was only from waking up. She looked at the clock: 7:46 a.m.

Jackson was fast asleep. She tried to remember if his face had been there among the others the night before. She could have sworn it was, but why? How? How could he have been at her side unless he'd already been at the bar?

She shifted, lifted her hand to the bandage on the side of her scalp. *Oh, God*, she thought. *Please don't let me look too messed up.* She had class at ten.

Class. She had to call Lawrence. Her hand clenched involuntarily, and Jackson lifted his head, focused two weary eyes on her.

"What is it? You okay?"

She nodded. "What are you doing here?"

"I followed the ambulance last night. Do you remember last night?"

"Yes. Vaguely. You were there?"

"I was. So was Blake, or you might have been injured further."

"Are you angry?"

"With you? No." He cupped her face and kissed her. He pulled away at the sharp knock on the door. A nurse came into the room to bring her breakfast and check her vitals.

While she ate, Jackson sat in the chair next to the bed and talked on his cell phone to Lawrence. "Seven days," he said to Lawrence, glancing over at her with a look she couldn't place. Scorn, disappointment? Irritation? "Seven days before she'll be able to take class."

After that she could only pick at her food. Her life was falling apart. Injured at her second job, when she wasn't even really supposed to have a second job. If it got her fired from her first job, she was truly and thoroughly fucked.

"Is he mad?"

"You're so concerned about whether everyone is mad. How do you feel, Prosper?"

Her throat got tight. "Not very good. Kind of miserable, actually." Her voice wobbled on the last word.

His irritated expression softened. He sat on the bed beside her and drew her into his arms. "Go on, get it over with."

The kindness in his voice made her weep. He held her as she sobbed out her stress. His fingertips ran slowly up and down her arm, and the beat of his heart against her ear soothed her. When she finally calmed down, he turned her so she faced him and took her hand.

"Okay. Now I want you to listen. Lawrence isn't mad. I'm not mad, not at you. But this situation has to stop. You can't work at a bar three nights a week until three in the morning, especially if bar fights are going to land you in the hospital with eight stitches in your head. You're supposed to be dancing for Lawrence. For me. This other stuff is—" He made an impatient gesture. "Don't you have any family to help you? Any cheaper place to live?"

"I've asked. Everyone already has roommates. I could probably find a cheaper place farther out, but I don't want to take the subway at night—and I can't afford a car—" She sighed and dropped her head in her hands. "And my mom... I just can't..."

"Why not?"

Prosper rubbed her eyes. "I don't want to think about it."

"You need to think about it. You need to find a place to live."

"I have a place to live."

"A safe place. Your building is a few weeks away from being condemned."

She looked up at Jackson. "Just please stop looking at me that way."

"What way?"

"Like I'm a total fuckup. I know I am. And you witnessing all of it only makes it worse."

"Prosper—"

"I don't want to stop dancing. I don't want to leave New York. I'll figure it out. I just need some time—"

"Prosper—"

"What?"

"Come live with me for a while. Until you get back on your feet."

She went very still, shocked that he would suggest it. She wanted so much to jump at his offer, but at the same time she had so many questions and doubts. How would it work? Did he really want her to move in? Was he just guilty about what had happened? She tried to phrase a coherent response to his suggestion, but only garbled questions came out.

"But I... What... How..."

"There would be some things to work out. Obviously. But it seems like the most logical thing to do under the circumstances. I'm tired of worrying about you, and you're working way too hard. And to be honest, I would enjoy having more time with you. Outside of work."

"More time?" He wanted more time with her. She tried not to look too excited about that in the face of his casual tone. "Playtime, you mean?"

He shrugged and looked away. "If that's what you want to call it. You-and-me time. But the rest of the time is my time. You can move in, but I'm not going to play the happy nice boyfriend, okay? And it goes both ways. You don't have to spend any more time with me than you want to."

"So we would be like roommates with benefits?"

He chuckled. "Sure. I guess."

"I...well...I don't want to put you out. When we started all this, you said no commitment. I know you don't really want a roommate."

He was quiet a moment before he answered her. "You're right. A roommate isn't exactly what I want. But it's unfair to ask you for the other thing. Not as a condition to move in, anyway."

"What other thing?"

He took a deep breath. "A deeper relationship. On the D/s side. More in-depth interaction."

"More in-depth interaction? Meaning what?"

"More obedience, more pain, more restrictions, more intimacy. More everything, Prosper. For better or worse, you make me crave more. But I'm not going to pin that on as a requirement of room and board. I'm allowing you to move in as a friend, as someone who has an interest in your well-being. The rest..." He shrugged. "That would be up to you."

She hesitated only a moment. "Yes."

"Yes, what?"

"Yes to more. I want more too."

He frowned. "You just had a head injury, and you're in a hospital bed. You might not be thinking things through as well as you should."

"No, I know I want more. If you show me, if you explain to me what you want—"

He put a finger over her lips. "First things first. You need to get yourself better. We'll get you moved in, and then you need to recuperate and rest. Seven days of bed rest, the doctor said, before you try any strenuous dancing again. Or any strenuous decisions. Okay? Seven days. I should make it two weeks, but I suppose I don't have much more self-control than you."

Prosper stared at the clear blue eyes across from her, the usually stern face that had relaxed suddenly into easier lines. Or was it only that she knew him better, to see the ease around his mouth, his eyes?

"What?" he asked.

"Thank you, Jackson. For a place to stay. For being here now."

He shrugged and squeezed her hand again. "Just remember, it's not completely unselfish. None of this is completely unselfish."

Prosper shrugged too and said, "It never is."

Jackson had helped her home, carried her up the last two flights of stairs when she was too tired to climb them herself. To her amazement he hadn't even been winded at the top. He'd helped her get settled into bed, tucking the sheets around her closely. His careful protectiveness fueled the slow burn in her heart—and her more private parts too. He'd told her to rest, that he'd return later to help her pack. His exact words were, "Do not dare try to do it yourself." She'd packed a little anyway when she found she couldn't lie still. She'd fallen back into bed a half hour later wishing she'd obeyed Jackson. By the time he returned, her head felt better, but he scowled at the small boxes of belongings.

"I told you to rest."

"I know. I got bored."

In the space of a second, he was across her bedroom and in her face.

"You got bored? That's enough of an excuse, girl? What did I tell you to do?"

"Rest," she whispered.

"Rest, Sir."

"Rest, Sir," she managed despite the sudden erratic beating of her heart. "You told me to rest. I'm sorry."

"If you want more, Prosper, you'll have to give more. You'll have to keep your mind on what I want, not your own needs."

"Yes, Sir."

He put a hand to her forehead. "How do you feel? Any fever? Dizziness, headache?"

"A small headache, nothing bad. The nurse said I might have them off and on for a few days."

"If it gets worse, you'll let me know." It was an order.

"Yes, Sir."

He finished packing the boxes for her. It both thrilled and embarrassed her to watch him handling her things, all her things, down to her toiletries, her pajamas, her naughty bras and panties. She blushed at the intimacy, but he was very businesslike about it. While he carried her things downstairs, she wrote a check for two weeks' rent to the landlord to close her lease. With any luck there would be units available when her time at Jackson's house was finished, but she didn't want to dwell on that now. She wanted to enjoy every moment she had with him and not worry about what came after.

At his house, he brought in her things while she watched from the sofa. She thought of the early days when she'd come over, of the time he'd bent her over that same couch and spanked her with his belt.

When would he touch her again? He seemed determined that she rest, but she was in anything but a restful mood.

He made a light dinner of chicken and salad, and they ate it together at his small dinette. The apartment was dark as always, the only faint light the fixture over their heads. She joked that he lived like a vampire, afraid of light and sun.

"Perhaps," he replied. "And you're coming to stay with me. Here in my lair." He reached out for a lock of her hair. "Little sunshine," he said in a quiet voice.

She looked up at him in the dim light. She was so in love. So desperately in love with him. And the way he was looking at her... His eyes looked darker than usual, more intent. He didn't let go of her hair, only caught a greater handful and twisted it in his fist. "You didn't obey me earlier, girl."

She was silent, her breath expanding in her chest. Her heart seized hopefully. *Please touch me. Please.*

"How are you feeling?" His voice sounded strained. "Any headache? Any pain?"

"No. I'm fine."

"You should really be getting to bed soon. You need to be resting as much as possible. But I think you earned a punishment earlier. For disobeying me."

She nodded. "Yes, Sir. If you say so."

He released her hair with a soft laugh. "Good answer. Now get up. Bend over the table. Wait for me."

She was throbbing, just like that. Three short commands and she was soaking her panties. She stood and draped herself over the small table while he cleared the dishes. Her face flamed with the indignity of what she was doing, waiting there bent over for him as he moved around her. She heard water running in the kitchen, things being put away. The dishwasher started with a hiss and a groan. She turned her head sideways and closed her eyes, too embarrassed to see if he watched her or not. Her hands opened and closed against the tabletop. Her fingers traced across the smooth wood. She wished it were Jackson's skin.

She heard footsteps and opened her eyes to see him coming back, wiping his hands on a dishtowel. He threw it aside and approached her. She loved the way his jeans eased across the muscles of his thighs when he walked. Her whole pelvis ached with lust for him.

He stood behind her, reached around to unbutton her jeans and tug them down over her hips. She held her breath, waiting, feeling exposed. The panties came down too. She shifted and buried her face in her hands. She was overcome with the same jumble of feelings he always inspired in her. Lust. Fear. Excitement. Embarrassment. Why did she love this? Why did he?

"Be still," he said under his breath. She shuddered as she heard a metallic clunk and the sound of his belt being freed from its loops. She craned her neck to turn and see him doubling it over. As always, she squelched the sudden impulse to flee. He took her hands hard and pulled them behind her back, pressing them down.

"When I tell you to do something or not do something, it's understood that you will obey. Yes?"

"Yes, Sir," she whispered.

"There will always be a reason, girl. And the reason will always be 'I want.' So if I give you directions, you do as I say and not as you want to do. Do you understand?"

"Yes, Sir."

"'Yes, Sir, I understand.'"

"Yes, Sir, I understand." She tensed as he rubbed the belt across her ass cheeks.

He leaned down next to her ear. "This won't hurt you nearly as much as it should, because you're injured. Now count each stroke and don't dare move."

He brought the belt down on her bottom, and she gasped. "One!"

The sting of the first blow spread across her cheeks. He paused then, making her wait. She felt so vulnerable knowing more pain was coming. She both dreaded the pain and yet craved it on some level just because it came at his hands.

"Two! Three! Four!"

They weren't full strength, as promised, but they still hurt. He swung the belt with tight control, and the hard table held her trapped with nowhere to go. She danced around on her toes, trying to dissipate some of the ache. Her ass grew warm and tender, but at the same time a different type of warmth suffused her pussy. She tensed, aware of her nipples hardening into stones against the tabletop. She wanted to press her clit against the edge, but she didn't dare. Even through the haze of pain, she was reminded of his power and control of her by the hand on her back, the fingers tight on her wrists. She struggled just to feel him hold her harder. He didn't stop the steady delivery of blows, each one another trial to endure, another slap of fire. On top of all the other warring emotions and sensations, she had to remember to count each one. "Five! Six! Seven!"

"Eight!" was the last. He put the belt down on the table and helped her up. She swallowed hard and looked up into his eyes, feeling ashamed and aroused. Or perhaps ashamed because she felt so aroused. His gaze was direct and stern, and for a moment she had difficulty finding her voice.

• *137* •

"I'm so sorry, Sir. Next time I'll do what you say, I promise."

"Every time you'll do what I say. Okay? And if you can't, you'll let me know, and you'll explain to me why."

"Yes, Sir."

"Are you tired, girl?"

"Yes. I'm very tired."

He put a hand under her elbow. "Then let's get you to bed."

He led her straight to his bedroom. He shouldn't have. She was tired, and she was supposed to be recuperating. There was a second bedroom where he'd put all her things earlier, but that room was on the top floor, and he didn't want her that far away. She was an invalid. She needed supervising. That's what he told himself anyway. He sent her to shower, lingering outside the bathroom in case she got dizzy and fell, then gave up and joined her, drinking the water from her luscious skin.

He should never have moved her into his house. He wouldn't be able to leave her alone.

When she got out of the shower, he forbade her to put on pajamas. He didn't want her body covered from his gaze. He took her towel and nodded to the bed. "Left side." She walked over and climbed between his sheets, curled up there, not a lost kitten anymore. He hung up the towel and came to join her. Once in bed, he pulled her close. She was so cold, and he noticed too that she felt thin. She really was run-down. Letting her move in was something he simply had to do for her health and safety. She needed looking after. And he needed her in his bed because...because... *Because you have to have her.*

She sighed and arched back against him.

"You need to rest," he said. But two seconds later he turned to the bedside drawer to get a condom and sheathe himself. He eased inside her with a slow, steady motion that would have been impossible to halt. She gasped as she always did when he first entered her, shifting her hips to adjust to his girth. Gasp turned to moan— hers or his, he didn't know. Both, perhaps. They moved together like that, slow and splendid, for what might have been an hour but probably wasn't. It was as if they sealed some new contract, some new promise. Deep feelings. Immense possibilities. *Prosperity.*

Later, when he held her sleeping body against his satiated one, he hoped against hope he hadn't made a mistake.

12 CHAPTER TWELVE

Prosper woke up alone to silence. No small, depressing apartment. No screaming and yelling from next door. Just silence and a wide, white bed. The diaphanous curtains undulated over semi-open blinds that let in bright morning light. The temperature was perfect, not too hot and not too cold, and Prosper stretched under the covers, pulling them up to her ears. She could smell Jackson.

Jackson.

Had he left for work already? She listened, thought perhaps she heard the rattle of a newspaper. She left the bed, padded to the door, and cracked it open. She went upstairs to the guest room to find her pajamas, and then tiptoed down the stairs. Why was she tiptoeing? Why did she feel like an intruder? She reached the bottom of the second flight and peered around the corner to see him sitting at the table over coffee, eggs, and bacon. Sunlight fell across his face as he mulled over the headlines. He rattled his paper again and put down his cup.

"You live here now, Prosper. You don't have to skulk around."

Her heart thumped at the sound of her name on his lips. He looked up and smiled, and beckoned her over. "Sit down." He nodded to the chair beside him. "I'll get you some breakfast." He stood and headed for the kitchen.

"I'm not hungry. I don't usually eat breakfast—"

The look he gave her as he passed made her voice trail off.

"In this house we eat breakfast. Sit."

She sat, her heart surging in her chest. *In this house we eat breakfast.* It sounded so domestic. *Don't get excited, it's just for now,* she reminded herself as she sat on the edge of the chair, then sank back into it. She stared at the table and blushed, remembered Jackson spanking her over it with his doubled-over belt. He chuckled as he set a plate of eggs, bacon, and toast in front of her.

"No room here for a dungeon to keep you properly in line. We use what we have. Don't we?"

She smiled up at him, her face on fire. "Yes, Sir." She picked at her eggs. "I... Do I...call you Sir? Here in your house? Now that I'm living here full-time?"

He shook his head with a slight frown. "We're not going to be full-time. I don't have the energy or inclination to do it. But you may call me Sir whenever we're alone if you like. Just don't forget and come out with it during rehearsals or something. People will have enough to talk about as it is."

"You'll tell them that I'm staying here?"

His frown deepened. "I won't tell anybody anything. But you know how dance companies operate. The gossip, the whispering. And Blake knows."

Prosper swallowed. "He does?"

"Not about the specifics, so you can start breathing again. But he knows we're together. He says he won't say anything, but…"

Prosper looked down in her lap. "One more reason for them to despise me. Believing I slept myself into the role." She looked up at Jackson, a horrible thought occurring to her. "Or maybe I did."

He shook his head. "You got that role based on your talent. Don't let anyone make you think otherwise." He waved his fork at her. "If I do anything before I leave here, I'll get you to understand how talented you are, that you deserve every success you get." He pointed at the bacon untouched on Prosper's plate. "Are you going to eat that?"

At her small shake, he took it and stuck it in his mouth, then stood up to take his plate to the kitchen. "I'm off. You stay in bed today and rest. Read a little, or watch some TV. There are DVDs next to the couch, naughty ones too." He smiled. "Watch them if you want. You might learn something. But Prosper"—his face rearranged itself into stern lines again, just like that. How did he do it?—"do not dream of doing anything else, unpacking, cleaning up. No dancing," he emphasized, pointing to her feet flexing under her chair. "Seven days of rest. Doctor's orders."

"I can't go seven days without dancing. You know I can't."

He cupped her face in his hand. "No dancing. Not full out. But if you like, when I get home and I can keep an eye on you, we'll have a little class." There was a glint in his eye she didn't miss. "Do you understand your directions, girl? I'm not kidding. When I get home, I'll know."

"Yes, Sir, I understand. But I really do feel okay."

His reproving look made her blush again. He lifted her from her chair, pulled her close, and kissed her, his smooth, morning-shaven skin a soft surprise.

"Be good. I expect you to be good."

Time in rehearsals dragged by. He felt a strange combination of contentment and agitation knowing Prosper was resting back at his home. He would have preferred if she was here, but she couldn't be, and really, how greedy could he be? She would be in his home until he left in the spring. He would see her at work, in practices, in *Firebird* performances starting in February. Life was good.

But practicalities dictated that he choose another girl to learn *Firebird* for now, to mark the steps in rehearsal as the other choreography went on, and he chose Elsa over Kristen only because he knew Kristen led the revolt against his girl. Kristen pouted so hard Jackson had to stifle laughter. He drew her aside to explain that, as the Tsarina, she was too indispensable to understudy the lead. Blake watched all of this with a cool detachment. If his allegiance to Kristen caused him to be irritated, he didn't show it. Jackson suspected he had more allegiance to Prosper than he let on.

And if Blake decided to cause problems for them, what would result? Jackson wasn't the first choreographer to romance a company dancer. Balanchine and Farrell were the stuff of every ballerina's dream. What would they do? Send him away? Hardly.

Their relationship bore absolutely no repercussions for him. Only for her.

He stuffed that thought down and concentrated on rehearsals, then left early for home. The streets were decorated for Christmas holidays, but his mind was full of *Firebird*. The choreography was all falling into place, although without Prosper it had been missing that special something that sent it over the top. Elsa made a miserable replacement. Her willowy limbs were unable to match the precision of Prosper's shorter, quicker legs. Thinking about her legs had him half aroused as he took the steps to the town house two at a time.

He let himself in and found her sleeping in his bed. He thought he should make her sleep in her own room, a way of preserving the power imbalance they both craved. But a part of him knew that was folly. They were like magnets. The pull had been there from the start, from the first moment he had seen her. Whatever explained it— pheromones, attraction, subconscious signals—the pull made it almost impossible for him to leave her alone.

But he did. She needed to rest, and he was pleased to find her resting as he'd ordered. He went into the kitchen and started to put together a simple dinner. He was already looking forward to watching her from across the small table, her smiles and gestures making the blood rush straight to his cock. *No, no, she needs rest. Seven days.*

He had other plans for tonight.

When dinner was on the table, he went in and crawled onto the bed next to her. She woke at once, and the sleepy, happy eyes she turned on him almost made him lose his resolve not to molest her. "You're being my good girl, yes? Resting?"

"Yes, Sir." She sighed and snuggled her warm body close to him.

"No, not now. Come on, cuddles. Dinnertime. Slowly, in case you're dizzy." He helped her up, but she insisted she hadn't felt dizzy all day. He supposed a dancer's brain would be least susceptible to dizziness, since a ballerina routinely spun in circles on one toe.

They sat and ate, and she had a decent appetite, ate nearly everything he gave her. He felt reassured that she was indeed up for a little class. He had fantasized about putting her through her paces privately since the first time he'd seen her dance, since the first time he'd seen her legs flex and her toes slide neatly across the floor. After dinner he had her sit and rest next to him on the couch while he wrote some e-mails on his laptop. Then he stood and pushed the furniture against the walls. She watched in silence, the only outward sign of excitement the clasping and unclasping of her hands.

"Here, girl." He pointed to the center of the floor. "Class time."

She hesitated.

"Will I need pointe shoes, Sir?"

"Of course you will. You'll also need to undress completely. I want to see your lines."

She took a deep breath at those words, then went for the shoes and returned. He watched with his arms crossed over his chest as she took off her pajamas, revealing the body he knew, the body he loved. The body that still struck him every time with its power and perfection.

"Shoes," he prompted, when she stood, still staring at him. Her mind was clearly as muddled with lust as his. Her fingers fumbled with the ribbons as she drew them up and around each ankle, tied them, and tucked the knots inside.

"Okay, up. First position." He took her through a short series of rudimentary exercises. *Pliés, chassés, battements, relevés.* He stood right in her dance space and scrutinized her form. If only she made a mistake, even a small one, he could smack her lovely bottom in reprimand, but she was perfect as always. He thought about making the exercises harder, the tempo faster, to purposely trip her up, but the practical part of his mind kept insisting on rest. Seven days of resting.

Maybe next week.

For now, once he'd warmed her up and watched her lovely, nude body work through the movements, he put on some music, some indie with a good strong beat. It wasn't the classical she was used to, but he'd seen her dancing to it in his head. He partnered her, fed her the steps as he thought of them. She performed flawlessly. Her little hand grasped his, and her body moved through space. When she leaned on him, he gave her perfect balance, his own solid strength.

Then he pulled her down with his heart full of desire and his limbs alive with lust for her. He spread her legs. He would only taste her; that wouldn't tax her too much. He would only slide his tongue over her pussy lips, up to her clit that bloomed under his kiss. She tasted so sweet; the scent of her triggered some deep animal impulse inside him. He sucked and stroked her and thrust his fingers inside her tight wetness. She moaned in response and twisted her fingers in his hair.

He could feel the exact moment she started climbing, and he pressed his tongue hard against her clit, moving it back and forth. She bucked as his fingers found and stroked her G-spot inside. Rest be damned. He feasted on her until she screamed her release. He reveled in the feeling of her walls clenching around his fingers and the soft satin of her pointe shoes sliding across his back.

Jackson woke before her the next morning. It was Sunday. No class, no rehearsals, no performances—a day of rest for them both. Well, rest in a certain sense of the word, he thought, watching her sleep. As it turned out, Jackson didn't leave the bed until long after noon.

No, he stayed and watched her sleep, adjusting his erection when it became too painful. When she began to stir, he leaned over and fingered her awake, preparing her to take his cock. She was quickly wet, and he slid his fingers through her pussy, gathering the moisture. He pressed one slippery digit down to rest against her asshole. She flinched and tensed.

"Okay, girl. Not this morning. But soon." She made a soft, scared noise that excited him. He fumbled with the condom wrapper, then gathered her close and plunged into her tight, hot pussy. He looked down at her, thrilled by the way her features softened and her mouth fell open as he fucked her. The pleasure he gave her was written all over her face. They moved together, and each time he slid into her, he felt closer and closer to her. Tension grew in his dick, his balls. Sensation threatened to overcome him. He pulled himself together and refocused on her. God, she was never more beautiful than when she let herself go, when she gave herself up to his ownership of her.

He felt her shake, felt her hips press up against him with urgency. As her excitement mounted, she closed her eyes and threw her head back. "Look at me," he said. "Look at me while I fuck you. I want you to see who's giving you pleasure."

She opened her eyes and gazed up at him, flushed and fuck drunk, but self-consciousness bloomed soon enough. It wouldn't do. He would have to train it out of her. He wanted her to be nothing less than an uninhibited, mindless slut in bed, her self-awareness a thing of the past. He flipped her over and reentered her from behind. He forced her to spread her legs wide when some self-protective instinct had her drawing them together.

"Let me fuck you. I'll do as I like to you, won't I?"

She moaned in tortured assent and opened to him. He held her hips hard and fucked her, glorying in his mastery of her. Her arching, helpless attempts to find her own pleasure drove him on all the more. He came with a growl, shuddering through his own nerve-bending orgasm. He purposely didn't let her come. Afterward he lay beside her and told her again, "Look at me."

She looked over, flushed and beautifully unsatisfied. "If you want to come, girl, you're going to have to come my way. There's no other way, is there?"

"No, Sir," she said, her gaze shying away.

"Look at me." His sharp tone drew her focus back to him. "I want to be able to touch you whenever and wherever I want and not have you flinch. I want you to talk to me about sex without blushing and looking away from me."

"I'm sorry. It's hard for me."

"I know, and you're not good at sex. I remember," he teased, then fixed her with a stern look. "I think a more focused training program is long overdue."

She swallowed. "Um…maybe."

"The correct answer is 'yes, Sir,'" he said, taking her face in his hand.

"Yes, Sir. Yes, please train me. I want to please you. I do, more than anything." Her eyes looked deep into his, and he felt again the magnetic connection to her. Each time it shook him more.

"Good girl." He released her and smoothed his fingers across her cheek. "Now, I'm not going to restrain you. You control yourself. I'm going to touch you—everywhere—and you're going to let me. Understood?"

"Yes, Sir."

"And every time you pull away or cringe or blush, that's one stroke of the crop."

"The crop?" Her eyes went wide.

"Yes, I know you've never felt the crop. It's about time you did. It hurts. So try, girl. Try your best." He slid his fingers down her belly to the warm, smooth opening between her legs. "I'm not going to hurt you. I'm going to make you feel good. If you let yourself go, I'll make you come. Do you want to come, girl?"

"Yes, Sir." Her words came out in a sigh.

"Then let me touch you."

He began the slow, intimate work of desensitizing her to inhibition and embarrassment. He played with her, fingered her, stroked her, explored every fold and crevice of her. She blushed red—he knew she couldn't help it—and dropped her eyes away. "That's one, girl." She looked back at him, a rebuke and a plea at once, but he only laughed. "Two. For looking at your dominant that way."

He kept on, fascinated. He loved watching the pleasure war with the self-consciousness behind her gaze. The earned strokes mounted— three, four, five, six, seven, eight—but she persevered and gradually he felt her open to him. Her submission seemed to deepen, the blushes replaced with the flush of heavy arousal. When he had her near the edge, he stopped, took one taut nipple in his fingers and pinched hard. Her eyes closed. She gasped and jerked away slightly. "Nine," he said, and her eyes popped open. He pinched harder, and her hand came to his. She stopped short of trying to stop him, but he hissed and said, "Ten. Put them over your head. Both of them."

Tears welled in her eyes as he pinched her other nipple, but she obeyed. She kept her hands open and limp on the pillow over her head.

"Please..."

"Please, Sir," he corrected. "Eleven. Am I hurting you, little one?"

"Yes, Sir." Another flinch and shake.

"Twelve. Lie still. Just accept what I do to you. Just take it. You're going to be fine, and this gives me pleasure. Hurting you." He saw the desire flaring alongside the pain in her eyes. Two sides of the same coin. "Breathe deep. I'll let go in a minute."

She held still, tense. It would obviously take more than one round of training, but he was already looking forward to future sessions.

"Okay," he said, releasing her. "Good girl." But from there he dove his fingers into her pussy, got them slick and wet, then pressed his fingertips against her asshole. He teased her there, poking in one fingertip, then two. She flinched and squeaked. She tensed herself against the intimate invasion, and within moments the count rose to fifteen. "Stay right there," he said.

He got up and crossed the room, rummaged in a drawer, and pulled out a small silver toy. He opened the bedside drawer to pull out a bottle of lubricant and drizzle it onto the toy while she watched wide-eyed.

"Turn over," he said when he returned. "On your hands and knees, ass up."

She swallowed, hesitated.

"Sixteen," he said. "Don't make me ask again."

She rolled over on all fours. Again he stifled a smile. She was one huge cringe.

"Seventeen. Head down."

She lowered her head to the bed. He knelt behind her and noticed she was actually shaking. He made some soothing noises and rubbed the small of her back. Then he used one hand to press her down, holding her still. "This is only a small plug. I want you to wear it for one hour. Believe me, this is for your own good, because I am going to use your asshole soon, and it will be uncomfortable for you, even with training. So be a good girl and open up for me."

He pressed it against her. Many moans, twitches, and flinches later, she was up to twenty-five strokes with the crop, but the lovely silver toy sticking out of her ass gave him a deep sexual response. His cock ached to be where the plug was. He wanted to be driving into her ass. Not yet. He leaned down over her, reached around to flick her clit and run his fingers over the tips of her nipples. She bucked at the lightest touch.

"Soon, girl. Not quite yet. How does that feel, the toy in your ass?"

She moaned, and he swatted her thigh.

"You're already getting twenty-five with the crop. Stop whining and answer properly. How does it feel?"

"It feels naughty, Sir," she finally managed. "It feels bad, but good."

"Like you, hmm?" His fingers began to move in slow circles around her clit. Her trembling increased, and she swallowed a gasp. He smiled. "I'm going to make you come now, before I punish you. Otherwise all you'll be thinking about is how horny you are. You are a horny slut, aren't you?"

Only the smallest pause, then, "Yes, Sir."

"Yes, Sir, I'm a horny slut."

"Yes, Sir, I'm a horny slut. Please, please, let me come!"

Lovely begging. He could feel her humming, drawn up tight under his hands. He could make her do any manner of things right now; she was so desperate to get the release he had thus far withheld. But he had tortured her enough.

He thrust his fingers inside her pussy, then drew the moisture downward to stroke across her engorged clit. He gloried in the helpless cries she couldn't stifle, the violent shudders that wracked her body. When he sensed she couldn't hold off any longer, he told her to come. He held her hands down to the bed as the orgasm possessed her. He felt her teeth open against the side of his hand, felt her tongue come out to taste his skin. She bit him. Not hard, but hard enough that his cock ached and he had to subdue the impulse to impale her. When he finally felt her go limp, he guided her down onto her tummy. He let her rest, stroking her damp skin. He enjoyed watching the tiny tremors that still shook her from time to time.

"Okay, girl," he finally said. She moaned as he got up and went to the closet. She looked back over her shoulder as he returned with the whippy crop in his hand. Gorgeous, submissive look. It made some wild thing inside him start to come unhinged. *Focus. Control.* He was determined to see the scene through, as much as he'd like to bury himself inside her at once. She twitched her bottom slightly to the side, the toy still shining between her cheeks. Nice try at distraction. He smiled and tapped the crop next to her face on the bed.

"You had your fun. Now I have mine."

She looked over at the thin black implement, too spent and sated to show much of a fear response. Girl goo. Beautiful. He sat beside her on the bed and began to stroke the whippy end of the crop up and down her silken back.

"We had some lessons today. Some training. What did you learn?"

"To let you touch me. To not flinch and blush."

"Hmm." He drew the end of the crop down between her legs and teased her there. "Are you blushing now?"

She hid her face. Decidedly blushing. He chuckled low in his throat. "As I suspected, it will take more than one session."

"I'm sorry, Sir," she said, and she sounded so truly sorry his cock ached.

He buried his hand in her hair, twisted it in his fingers. "Well, you'll learn." He stood and took up the crop. He gave a couple of tentative strokes. She cried out by the third stroke, and the fourth made her collapse on her side, her hands reaching back to cover her cheeks.

"Please!"

"Please what?"

"Please, Sir!" She drew out the *Sir* into a plaintive whine. He knew it hurt. He'd purposely waited until she'd orgasmed so there would be no sexual arousal to dampen the pain. When no safe word came, he went for restraints and tied her hands behind her back while she made little hiccupping sounds of distress. Then he decided to tie her around the waist to the bed, a project that involved lots of rope, lots of adjustment and readjustment until he had her perfectly secured. That is, secured enough to struggle a little but not to twist away. It was all worth it when he resumed, when he got to watch her dodge and fidget through the remaining twenty-one strokes, unable to pull away. She pleaded, "Please, please, please!" and with each plea he grew harder for her.

"Quiet, girl," he said. "Punishment hurts."

She didn't use a safe word even though he pushed her a little further along the pain continuum than he'd pushed her before. He wondered whether she didn't use it because she didn't need to or because she wanted to be the perfect submissive for him. He'd have to have a talk with her about the fine line between selflessness and self-preservation, about the dangers of perfectionism in S&M. He thought he was skilled enough to recognize her limits, but even the best of dominants erred sometimes.

Later. They'd talk later.

For now he dropped the crop, climbed on the bed behind her, held her sore red ass with the silver toy still shining between her cheeks. He stroked the welted, hot flesh and reached for the bedside drawer.

She was still tied down, and she was wild and wet. He ripped the condom open and rolled it on, then positioned himself at her pussy. She made a deep groaning sound and strained at the ropes, arching for him. All he could think of was the unbearable need to be inside her. He eased forward, his throbbing cock nudging against the toy in her other passage. The feeling of tightness was incredible. Double penetration. She loved it just as he expected she would. He noted her little hands making fists and felt her trembling just before he was lost to the world. She came within moments of him, howling and bucking, far, far too gone to ask permission first. Afterward he lay sprawled over her, spent and deeply satisfied. He didn't untie her for a long time.

CHAPTER THIRTEEN

"So Angie said she heard from Bucky that you were sharing an apartment with Jackson. Is that true?"

Glenna was desperately trying to get to the bottom of things, and Prosper felt awful for being secretive when Glenna had been such a good friend. But at the same time she couldn't let Glenna, the biggest gossip in the company, know what was going on with her and Jackson.

Unfortunately it was only her first day back at work, so she was too tired and disorganized to think on her feet. She grasped for a plausible, innocent explanation.

"He...he was at the bar when the accident happened. He doesn't want me to work now, after the head injury and everything. He wants me to concentrate on *Firebird*, so he's letting me stay in his guest room for free. But that's all it is. Just staying at his place. Like a roommate. I have my own room."

That wasn't a lie. She did have her own room, not that she ever used it. Glenna didn't have to know that.

"So you're totally living with Jackson Spencer. Is that what you're saying?" Her voice rose to a disbelieving squeak. "Basically you are totally living with him in his house! Just you and Jackson!"

Prosper laughed. "I know what it sounds like, but it's not like that. We're just…" She waved her hand. To say *we're just friends* would not be true. To say they were lovers would be more accurate, but she couldn't say that, not when she knew Glenna had been sent to get the gossip by the other dancers who watched from across the cafeteria. "He's just helping me out. That's all."

More truth. He was helping her. He was part lover, part life coach, part sadistic tormentor. His help took the form of patient reminders to eat healthy meals and rest, and instructions on how to be more proactive about reaching her goals. He made her create lists and timetables for progress. The torment came when he started calling her "girl." Training sessions, careful and exacting lessons on how to address him, to serve him, to please him sexually. She put her head on her hand, starting to daydream.

"Prosper!" Glenna said. "You can't just wave your hand like that! So what is he like? The real Jackson Spencer? Is he a slob? Does he have girls over? Is he a male slut? Does he have any weird, gross habits?"

Prosper's mind flicked to the night before when he'd collared and leashed her and made her suck his cock with the lead wound tightly around his fist. "No, nothing too weird."

"I can't believe it." Glenna sighed. "I'm so jealous. You have to try to get a peek at him naked. I want to know how he's hung."

"How he's hung?" Prosper echoed. She was undergoing training every night now because his cock was too big to fit in her ass. "If I see, Glenna, you'll be the first to know."

"Damn right," she said. "We all want to know."

Prosper looked over at the other dancers. What would they think if they knew? Would they even believe what was going on every day and night between them? It was hard to imagine it didn't show. She thought some of them saw it. Blake saw it.

Blake knew.

In rehearsals Blake was friendly and supportive. He partnered her carefully. They had grown to know each other very well—as dancers who danced together frequently do—gotten to know each other's weight and balance and particular quirks. They shared small jokes, sections of the dance where he pretended to drop her. They laughed over steps where she once kicked him accidentally that he never let her forget. But every so often she caught a look that gave her pause.

Later, her first night back at performance, he cornered her outside the dressing rooms.

"Did the doctor clear you to come back?"

"I was at rehearsal today, remember?"

"Rehearsal is one thing." He plucked at a piece of lint on her poufed tulle skirt. "This is a performance. You should be resting."

"I've been resting for two weeks. And this is just *Nutcracker*. Hopping back and forth in a line, traipsing in a circle. It's not hard."

He smirked. "Ooh la la. Now that you're Jackson's protégé, you're too good for the corps. I knew it would happen soon enough."

Was he teasing? Was he flirting with her?

"What do you want, Blake?" She looked past him to where the other dancers milled around waiting for stage calls.

"I just want to be sure you're okay. You hit your head pretty hard, and you're back at work already."

"I got cleared at the doctor's. Jackson insisted on it." She bit off the last word, cursing herself for bringing Jackson back into the conversation. She looked up at him sideways.

"Yeah, I know. Don't bother to blush. And to be honest, I think you're an idiot. But it's your life."

"It's not—It's just—We're just—"

Blake held up his hand. "I don't want to hear. You're lying anyway."

"I'm not lying. We're just... Look. I know he's just..."

"Just using you?"

"Mmm. Maybe. But I'm probably using him too."

"Well, if it makes you feel better to think that."

"I don't just think it. It's true. Not that it's any of your business, but we aren't really together."

"So if you aren't really together, then you could go out with me, couldn't you?"

"What are you talking about?"

"Go out. Have coffee. Or dinner and dancing. Just go for a walk."

She snorted. Now that she had a big "I'm okay with being used" label on her forehead, suddenly Blake wanted to get to know her better. "Have coffee? Go for a walk? Me and you? I'm sure your friends would choke on their spit."

"I don't care. Anyway, if you aren't really together, we should go out. Why not?"

"Whatever, Blake." Prosper dodged around him and hurried to the wings, hid herself in a sea of white tulle and rhinestone tiaras. Dinner and dancing? Had Blake taken to drinking before performances? She ground the toes of her pointe shoes into the ground and thought to herself that a year ago she would have jumped at the chance.

But that was a year ago. Now she moved through class, rehearsals, performances to the beat of his name in her head. *Jackson. Jackson. Jackson.* Sometimes he came to watch her perform in the evenings. She begged him not to tell her if he was coming, because if she knew he was in the audience, she could barely remember the steps. When he did stay, he watched her closely. If she made mistakes, he noted them, and she paid for them later over his lap.

"No!" Jackson yelled.

Firebird rehearsals continued as always every day after class. The choreography was almost set, but Jackson seemed more, not less, agitated as the days went by.

"No, try it again. Stop!"

Prosper dropped off pointe and crossed her arms over her chest. Blake glared at Jackson.

"No. There are three beats before the lift. You have three beats to throw yourself at him. You," he said, pointing to Prosper. "He doesn't run to you; you run to him. Stop being a pussy and do it."

"I was."

"You run at him like you expect him to miss you. Look at him! He's going to catch you. If he doesn't, we've got other problems to worry about."

Prosper pursed her lips and looked at Jackson. Moving in with him hadn't softened him toward her in the studio at all. He prodded; he railed. He demanded, and he dared her to fight back. She looked down at her pointe shoes. The ribbons were fraying, the satin by the toes was ripped. The boxes were soft from sweat. A mess, just like she was. She glanced up at him from under her lashes.

"Blake and I will work it out. It will take a few times."

"A few times?" Blake cut in, shaking his head. "This is a dangerous lift. Why can't I do a traditional overhead lift? Catch her by the waist, then overhead—"

"Because traditional is boring. I want you to catch her in flight. This is passionate, sexy. I want to feel excited when I watch this *pas de deux*. I want to see you subdue her to your will."

Prosper blushed. Damn it. Why was she still blushing over this? Jackson had talked to her a hundred times already about his ideas on the ballet, and now she couldn't look at it innocently, not anymore. He'd taken a traditional tale where the prince catches a Firebird and turned it into high D/s pornography, at least in her mind. After the new year they would begin practicing the entire work in preparation for the start of the spring season. This was the only section he kept changing. He kept making it more complex. More difficult. More dangerous.

"Catch, swing, turn her around, and catch her in your arms like this—" Jackson mimed a passionate bear hug.

Blake still looked doubtful. "If I miss the turn, if she swings even slightly off balance, she's hitting the floor! And she's going to be moving fast, she's going to be up in the air—"

Jackson waved a hand. "This is Prosper we're talking about. Perfect Prosper. She'll hit her mark. You just hit yours. I want it to look like you're catching a bird in midflight. And you," he said, spinning on her. "Stop being so afraid. We've talked about this before."

Jackson's ballet wasn't easy. Jackson wasn't easy. He pushed and pushed. He pushed her at home; he pushed her at rehearsals. Her feet ached, but worse, her nerves were shot. He walked over and took her arm to lead her back across the rehearsal room.

"Again. Head up. Run fast. You're trying to get away. I want to see fear in your face and panic in your body. Let Blake partner you. Work with him. And Blake, you control her. You've caught her. She's yours. Show me in your face how that makes you feel. Show me how you make her give up her freedom for you."

Prosper squared her shoulders and took a deep breath. Blake stood, waiting. She ran; she leaped. He caught her in a grasp that hurt her, swung her over his head high in the air. His hands left her. Free of the earth, she arced upward for a millisecond, then came down. She squeaked as his strong arms gripped her. He hugged her as Jackson had demonstrated. It felt crushing. Her toes just skimmed the floor.

"Okay," said Jackson. "Was that so hard? Repeat five hundred times and make it bone memory. The audience will gasp. It will all be worthwhile." He looked down at his dance book, already moving on to other steps. Prosper thought he thought she could do anything in the world. She wasn't so sure.

"Jackson," she said. "If I slip, if we get it wrong, I'll fall on my back. Or if he drops me in the catch afterwards, I'll snap one or both of my ankles."

"That's ballet, isn't it, girl?" Jackson looked up at her, unwavering. "If you don't want to get hurt, don't get it wrong."

They walked home together later that night. Jackson was quiet, but that wasn't unusual. Rehearsals had gone well aside from her abiding anxiety about the lift. She and Blake had tried it fifteen times in a row afterward, until the skin he grasped at her waist was so raw and sore she had to bite her tongue to keep from crying out. It wasn't bad partnering to grab her that way. It was good partnering. Clutching, good. Dropping, bad.

And Prosper fought her own fears to make it work every time. Tensing or shrinking during a lift could make a slight dancer unliftable, while good balance and propulsion could make a heavy dancer effortless to lift. Partnering in general was such a complicated and precise art, but lifts even more so. The female had to keep her abdominals tight, but her body loose. She had to keep herself perfectly centered in space but not rigid. The man provided the muscle and the counterbalance in the event of a waver. The male had to learn with each female he partnered how to guide her particular body to the right axis in space. With the best pairings it developed naturally, almost like falling in love. With others it was a struggle. It was a conscious effort to adjust the balance each time.

She looked over at Jackson, head down, shoulders hunched against the bitter December wind. It was almost Christmas, and while the decorations and twinkling lights of the neighboring townhomes were lovely, they did nothing to take the edge off the frigid wind. She suppressed a shiver. He took his scarf off and wrapped it around her shoulders.

"I told you to start dressing more warmly. This isn't peacoat weather. Especially when you weigh ninety-five pounds."

Prosper weighed more than ninety-five, but not by much. She'd begun to lose weight, not by any real effort, just the punishing performance and rehearsal schedule at this time of year. And yes, every so often, she decided not to eat. She liked to feel light, empty. It was easier to dance that way. But she knew she had to maintain her weight. Her clothes were getting loose, and she'd been fitted already for her Firebird costume. If she lost or gained weight, even a little, the tight silhouette wouldn't fit right.

Unfortunately, when she was at the apartment with Jackson, food was the furthest thing from her mind. Even now, during this silent, tense walk to Jackson's street, when they didn't touch for fear of being seen, she burned for him. He'd made her his Firebird, but more than that, he'd lit her up. He'd set her on fire.

At the Townsend, they worked. They collaborated. At his apartment, he took her in his arms and everything else fell away. There was only his naked, golden skin and his heavy cock in her hands, between her legs. Hairy chest against her smooth one, strong knees pushing her thighs apart, arms she was powerless to escape. Hard hands that pinned her down and a gaze that could pin her down even harder. Softly whispered directions, barked commands. Rough fingertips exploring her skin.

He glanced over as if he could tell what she was thinking. She might have had flames licking out of her ears from the thoughts in her head. Maybe he was thinking similar thoughts. *Two more blocks. Two more.*

"Talk to me about the lift, Prosper."

Okay, maybe not thinking similar thoughts. She pulled her peacoat around her more snugly and nestled her face into Jackson's scarf. It smelled like him. Aftershave? The soap he used? She would steal this scarf, hide it so when he was gone she would still have it to remember him by. Remember his smell, remember the way he wrapped it around her whenever she shivered.

"Prosper." He was looking over at her. She pulled her nose from its soft, fragrant haven.

"I'll get it. It's just a little scary."

"Is it because you don't trust Blake?"

"I trust Blake."

"Don't tell me lies. Look at me. Do you trust Blake?"

She did a small half shake of her head and shrugged again. It was too complicated to explain. "I mean, I do trust him—"

"Has Blake hit on you?"

That question she did not expect. She looked over at him with a frown. "Would you care if he did?"

"Has he or hasn't he?"

"Once. A couple of weeks ago."

"What did you say?"

She shook her head. "Nothing. We never even finished the conversation. I think he was joking."

"I doubt that."

They both fell silent.

"About you and me, Prosper... Everything's still okay?"

She took a deep breath. Her palms were starting to sweat. "What do you mean?"

"You're enjoying living with me? You don't want to move out?"

She didn't even have to think about it. "No, Jackson. Not at all."

"I know I'm hard on you at work. And I ask a lot of you at home too." He stopped, and she looked over at him. Their breaths intermingled, white and wispy, in the air between them.

"I just want you to know..." He paused and shifted, rubbed his lip. "That lift. I know it seems hard right now. But you'll get it."

She swallowed. *Half a block.*

"Yeah. Yes, I will. Can we go home now? I'm really starting to feel the cold."

At dinner they talked about Christmas. *Nutcracker* would continue until the first week of January, so Prosper couldn't get away. Jackson could, and planned to visit his family and friends back in Chicago. Prosper knew he felt guilty about leaving her behind at the holidays. And to be honest, the idea of it upset her. Sure, she could spend the night of Christmas Eve after the performance with her dancer friends. Partying, drinking. She could sleep late on Christmas morning, do whatever she wanted. But she'd be doing it without him.

Still, she had known. He had an entire life back in Chicago, and her life was here. She had a job that required her to perform, a contract. He could take two weeks away; she couldn't.

While they talked about the holidays, he had asked questions about her family. Prosper didn't have much to say that he would understand. Apparently he came from a healthy family, a family that wanted to be together for the holidays. He had two brothers and two sisters, seven nieces and nephews, and parents who still followed the holiday traditions of his youth. He described Christmas Eve with his family, football and pizza for the guys while the women baked cookies for Christmas Day. Later they hung up stockings and sang holiday songs with the little ones. He described it all with such enthusiasm and detail, Prosper almost felt herself there.

Prosper had long since gotten over the fact that her family was different. She had an entire part of her family and history living far away on some Amish farmland, completely uncaring that she was alive. The family she did have, she had broken with for complex reasons that she couldn't share with him, that she couldn't share with anyone. Dance was her family now, the other dancers her siblings. The company was her parent, and the theater was her home.

And Jackson was her life. Two weeks without him. Merry Christmas and happy New Year.

After dinner she wanted to forget about the holidays, forget about the fact that he was going away. She felt grouchy and emotional. She wanted him to hurt her so she could bawl the way she wanted to and he wouldn't know it was because of him. He put his elbows on the table and looked over at her. She rolled up her napkin and placed it next to her plate and waited, as she did every night, for directions.

"Clothes off and go stand facing the wall. That wall," he specified, pointing to the far side of the living room. Familiar emotions assailed her. Shame, nervousness, and hot, shivery arousal. She stood and undressed, then walked to the opposite wall, hyperaware of her nudity. She kept her hands at her sides as she'd been taught. No covering up. When she reached the wall, she stood against it, her nipples and knees touching the cool white-painted surface as Jackson required. She heard him leave the room, go up the stairs. A moment later she heard him padding back down.

She jumped when he put his hand on her hip. The thick carpet muffled everything. His other hand parted her ass cheeks and probed there. She blushed and burned, but she didn't dare pull away or make any defensive movements. The hand left, then returned. She felt cold lube shoved up inside her. He played with her ass a lot, training it, he said. He seemed to believe he'd be able to fuck her there one day, but she was doubtful. He was big; she was small.

Ouch. *Ouch.* Speaking of big, the toy he was pressing against her was stretching her painfully. She moaned, frightened of being hurt. He withdrew it, but it was only temporary relief, because next time he drove it a little deeper. In, out, increasing its forward progress in small increments until he finally drove it home. It was the biggest plug he'd ever used on her, and she felt it inside her like some unwelcome invader. Her ass ached as she clenched around the toy, unable to relieve the unnatural feeling of fullness. He pressed on it for good measure so she shuddered, and then he kissed her shoulder. She wanted to look back at him, to question him, to be soothed by him, but she knew her eyes were supposed to stay forward. She stared at the white wall and then felt something ticklish trail down her back. It took a while for her to place the sensation. Frayed rope.

"Give me your hands."

It was a relief to hear him speak. She thrust her hands behind her back.

"No, over your head. Cross your wrists behind the back of your neck."

She reached up and back, crossing her wrists as he'd told her to. The itchy-soft rope slid down her forearms, a sensory tease that made the hair rise on the back of her neck. He wrapped each wrist three or four times, then drew them together, letting out the rope a little. She felt a tugging as the two lengths of rope securing her wrists were pulled down and wrapped around the front of her waist, then around back again, and pulled snug. She felt him manipulating the rope in the middle of her back, cinching the ropes together, then felt both lengths drop down between her buttocks, over the flange of the toy stuck in her ass.

She held her breath as his hands came around the front. What he was doing to her felt so novel. No one had ever played with her this way, teasing and trussing her up so slowly and with such intent care.

His fingers played over her skin in soft tickly caresses as he moved the rope and formed the knots. Each light touch aroused her, sent frissons of lust arcing through her veins. She knew she couldn't look away from the wall, but she was sure the expression on his face was similar to the expression he wore in the studio when he was pushing her into this position or that, looking for that perfect arch or *port de bras*. She loved his face when it looked that way, how he looked when he was bringing his visions to life. She imagined herself as his canvas, his sculpture, his work of art.

She subdued the animal urge to grind her hips and stood still like a statue as he drew the ropes up between her legs, parting her ass cheeks so the rope rested right against the toy. He stopped and knelt beside her, then pushed her out from the wall. She stole a look down and saw him making a loose knot in the ropes, his mouth pursed in concentration. When he finished, he slid the knot between her pussy lips. Her breath was coming in little gasps. What he was doing to her had her so turned on she was afraid her legs would give out. She wanted to arch into the knot, relieve some of the erotic tension she was feeling, but she didn't dare.

He stopped and frowned, apparently unsatisfied with the placement. He pulled the rope away and adjusted it twice more until the knot rested squarely on her clit. She was going to shame herself in a minute and come without permission. She was humiliated by the wetness that must have coated his fingers and surely soaked the rope.

He gave it a good tug in front. She felt the toy bob in her ass, felt the scratching pressure on her clit and pussy lips, and moaned. He ignored her, leaning to secure the ropes over the crossed area at the front of her waist. He stood and looked at her.

"How does that feel?"

She wanted to answer but found herself only able to pant.

"That good? I'm glad you're comfortable. I have a few things to do before I get back to you." He turned her so she faced out into the room and walked away.

She stood, throbbing, melting. A quick test of her bonds revealed the devious efficacy of his design. The slightest shift to relieve the strain on her arms resulted in the rope between her legs being pulled more tightly, driving the toy in her ass deeper, the knot more firmly against her clit. She spread her legs, but it didn't help. It only made things worse.

She glanced over at Jackson clearing the table and was quite certain she saw a smile on his face. Sadist. It was impossible to stand still, but more impossible to bear the aching tease of arousal that resulted every time she moved. How long would he make her wait this way, tied and sopping wet between the legs?

It was far longer than she thought she could bear. Jackson cleaned the kitchen, then wrapped a few presents. He spent some time on the computer while she watched and tried to stand still. Finally he shut down his program and turned to her. He sat back in his chair and watched in silence from across the room. His intent gaze made it even more difficult not to pull and strain at the ropes that held her fast.

Please, please, she thought. *Please don't make me tell you how I feel.* She couldn't put it into words, how strong her feelings were for him. Strong enough to make the rope that held her obsolete. He held her with something much more inescapable than the knotted rope.

When he shoved back his chair and crossed to her, shedding his clothes, she breathed a sigh of relief.

CHAPTER FOURTEEN

His hands came around her waist and tugged at the rope so her clit throbbed.

"Do you want to come, girl?"

She tried to communicate the depth of arousal she felt in the only two words she was permitted at times like this. "Yes, Sir."

"I bet you do." He tugged at the rope again, and she moaned out a plea. "Down."

He helped her kneel, her arms still cinched behind her neck, her pussy still bisected by the unforgiving rope. Her ass clenched around the toy as he backed her against the wall. Her elbows and head were braced back against it, and she teetered on her knees, finding a center of balance. When she was steady, he left to sheathe himself, then returned and stood before her. He trapped her against the wall and brought his cock to her lips. She opened for him, running her tongue around the swollen head, exploring the familiar dimensions. The latex felt slick as she traced the ridge along the underside of his shaft. He groaned and leaned against the wall on one hand, twisting the other in her hair. He drove into her mouth, and she was powerless to stop him, not that she wanted to. She opened her mouth and throat for his pleasure.

Over time he'd trained a lot of the gag reflex out of her, so she only rarely choked and spluttered. Her arms, though, ached as his thrusts pushed her harder against the wall. She felt helpless and trapped, but then felt the emotional release, the easing of fear and the welcome tumble into subspace.

The rope knot was pulled back and forth across her clit with each thrust; rough, inescapable stimulation reminding her constantly of her predicament. His cock found the back of her throat, filling her senses with his masculine smell and closeness. Her thighs began to ache from tensing and untensing as the knot stimulated her clit. She moaned, the pleasure of the scratch and slide was so acute. Her moans against his cock seemed to drive him, and he began fucking her face. The knot against her clit tortured and teased her. Her hips jerked against it, seeking more. She was so close, so close!

His fingers tightened in her hair. "No. Don't dare."

She tried to distract herself, nearly insane from hovering at the edge of a release she wasn't allowed to reach. Soon afterward he growled and drove deep in her throat, shooting his load. She waited, barely remembering to be still and patient with his cock in her mouth as he'd taught her. *Obey. Submit.* But she wanted so much more, so much more she was almost insane. He eased out of her mouth with a sigh, then lifted her to her feet, grinning down at her. No doubt her desperation was written all over her face. His hand grasped between her legs, pulling at the knot again, pushing it against her clit.

"Please!" She begged for respite.

"What? You want to come, girl?"

"Yes, please, Sir. Please, I really do!"

He pulled her forward with her pussy lips cupped in his hand, leaned close so his hot breath was in her ear.

"There is only one way you're coming tonight, and that's with my cock buried deep inside your ass. Do you understand?"

She moaned.

"Do you understand, girl? Answer me."

"Yes!"

"'Yes, Sir. I can only come tonight with your cock in my ass.'"

"Yes, Sir, I can only come tonight with your cock in my ass. Please!"

"Don't worry. You'll get what you're begging for. Upstairs. Come on."

He took her up to the bedroom still trussed in rope and made her kneel, then pushed her forward until she was hunched over, her knees drawn into her chest. Then he checked all the ropes for tautness, his soft touches like fire trails burning on her skin. Again she felt the ache in her arms, and the more visceral, scary-hot feeling of restricted movement and powerlessness in his hands.

When he was satisfied with her position and the rope placement, particularly the placement of the knot against her clit, he picked up a flogger and heated her skin all over, from her back down to her ass. The evil leather strips wrapped around the bottom of her ass cheeks and made her jump from the sharp licks of pain. Each time she tensed and pulled her arms down, the rope dug into her molten center. The plug still spread her wide open. All the sensations built and merged inside her. She was wild to take his cock, to feel him fucking her. Her shrieks and yelps at the flogging soon turned to a drawn-out whine of despair.

"Please!"

He held the flogger still. "Please what, girl?"

She bit her lip and wiggled her ass. He brought the flogger down on the moving target, and she drew her knees in even more tightly against her chest with a low moan. She felt overpowered with lust, defeated by the ropes that held and tormented her as surely as he did. He had conquered her, and all the power was his. She was beyond dignity, beyond decorum. "Please...please—"

Again the tails bit into her, the inside of her thighs this time. "Try again. Tell me what you want."

"Please...please! Your cock—"

"'Please fuck my ass, Sir' will work nicely for me."

"Please fuck my ass, Sir!" she begged. "Please!"

She heard him drop the flogger on the nightstand and get a condom from the drawer. She shivered with excitement and fear as she waited for him. Would it hurt? The training was over. He was going to take her there now, in that tiny tight hole, and she had no way to stop him.

He knelt beside her and felt for the knot at the front and unwound it. As the knot fell away from her clit, he ran his fingers over it so her hips jerked. He flipped the rope up over her back, loosening the other knots so her arms fell forward to brace on the floor. She groaned as the large toy was withdrawn from her ass and more lube deposited in its place. It was so humiliating, but she was past the point of caring.

If she didn't get to come, she would die. He took her hips and touched his cock to her narrow opening.

"Just relax." He held her still with one hand on her neck while the other guided him into her farther, farther. The pain was immediate. She tensed and tried to pull away. He made a sound of frustration and withdrew. She felt more cold lube and, again, the pressure of his cock against her asshole. His hand kneaded her hip, her sore bottom cheek. "Open for me. Let me fuck your ass, and I'll let you come."

"I can't!" It hurt so much more than she'd expected.

"I won't hurt you. Just let it happen. It will hurt a lot less once it's in." As he spoke, he worked the head in deeper. Again she tensed, but he stayed still in her, his hands on both her hips now. "Wait, girl. Just...wait."

She waited. It was true; she wasn't dying. She was adjusting to him. She could feel herself relax around him. She felt her body begin to loosen, accept the inescapable invasion.

"Okay?"

In answer, she arched her hips a little. It didn't hurt anymore. No pain, just an incredible feeling of fullness. He drove deeper, little by little, every inch of his cock a revelation to her of just how deeply she could submit. He let out his breath in a gasp, withdrew, and fell forward again, sliding in all the way to the hilt. She clenched her fists and arched back against him. She basked in every sensation—the warmth of his front against her back, the hardness of his stomach trapping her, his fingers digging into her hips. His thick cock opened her up again and again, a steady invasion and sharp, erotic burn that gave her a sense of both vulnerability and fulfillment.

She was completely trapped. Her arms were useless, clipped wings. She was his, captured and subdued. He was inside her, splitting her open, advancing and withdrawing, subjugating her from the inside out. The tension that had gathered around her clit suffused her entire center and radiated up to her nipples.

"Oh, oh...please!"

He reached under her and found one hard nipple, twisted and pulled it between his fingers. The tension in her pelvis became a throb. Her ass clenched around his dick, and she collapsed onto her stomach. He drove into her, pulling her hair as she ground her clit against the floor, making noises like an animal. She felt fire and shattering drumbeat pulses through every nerve and vein. Her blood thrummed with a furious, erratic rhythm, and then she felt the sudden rush of completion, the release of all her pent-up, anguished lust. The walls of her ass contracted again and again on his dick. The intensity of the orgasm astounded her, turned her inside out. She gasped, unable to think or vocalize as the waves of pleasure took her. Then the sharp climax ebbed into a slow slide of aftershocks, leaving her feeling limp and replete.

She hadn't asked permission. She had been powerless to do anything at all. She rested, still impaled by his cock as he reached his own orgasm. Her skin slid across the scratchy carpet as he pumped against her, pummeling her hard with strong hips and thighs. She didn't brace or make any move to evade him in his forceful climax. She just let herself exist, drifting, glowing, conquered by the power of his lust.

The days flew by. Time seemed to slip through her fingers. Class was suspended the week before Christmas for twice-a-day performances of *Nutcracker*, although *Firebird* rehearsals still went on between shows. The set pieces began to arrive, and Prosper saw the technicians in the wings working on the orange and copper backdrops. A large apple tree that figured into Act One was rigged to glow with lights in the darkness of the twelve princesses' dance.

Prosper worked less as Jackson fine-tuned the other dances, and she had no part at all in the final act, when Blake, as Prince Ivan, and Kristen, as the Tsarina, had a glittering wedding amid the climactic fanfare of Stravinsky's score.

She haunted the backstage and watched Jackson interact with the others. She could tell he was excited to finally be seeing the ballet in its final form. She was excited too, but increasingly nervous. The costume arrived and had to be taken in, to the cluckings of the costume mistress. Jackson frowned over it but didn't lecture. She posed for the publicity photos in full costume and makeup with a great plume of red feathers decorating her hair.

Finally the day arrived when Jackson left for Chicago. He wouldn't let her drive him to the airport but left straight from rehearsals. That night after the performance, she broke down in the dressing room and cried. By now only Glenna spoke to her regularly. The company gossips had decided that yes, she and Jackson were a couple, albeit a secret one. The secrecy seemed to irritate them more. Some were jealous and snide because of it. Others looked down on her with holier-than-thou derision. With Jackson leaving her behind for the holidays, she looked all the more pathetic to those who judged her. Kristen was in her element, rallying the entire company against her. In the dance world, sleeping your way into roles was considered playing dirty. Well, they had no idea how dirty things really were.

Prosper tried to push it all from her mind. She couldn't go back. She couldn't change how things were. And she couldn't change the future, change the fact that he would leave her soon, leave her behind in this company where everyone, even the director, seemed to hate her. She couldn't think about any of it, because it all upset her too much. She thought about asking Jackson to take her to Chicago. She needed a change, needed a new direction.

She needed *him*.

She was falling apart without him. She couldn't eat; she couldn't sleep. Whenever he called, she pretended everything was fine because she didn't want to ruin his holidays. But without him, without his strength and encouragement, she began to be tortured by doubt. She became more and more certain she couldn't handle his ballet. What on earth was she thinking? She'd never be able to pull it off. When she royally fucked it up, he'd be furious with her. They would part on bad terms, and she'd be alone.

The days crawled along in a blur. At last it was New Year's Eve. Jackson would return on the third of January, if she could just survive until then. And after two final performances of *Nutcracker* on New Year's Day, she could hang up her long tulle tutu until next year. Everyone was tired of *Nutcracker*, and she was so worn out that her costume was practically hanging on her. She had to cinch it in with needle and thread.

The dancers of Townsend, from highest principal to lowliest corps, traditionally celebrated their own "New Year" the night of New Year's Day when the curtain came down on the final performance. Prosper thought she would go to the party. No matter what they thought of her, she was a member of the company too. She was as relieved about the end of *Nutcracker* as the rest of them. She would go and hold her head up, as Jackson always told her to do.

She would go because she was so lonely that even being at a party of people who hated her was better than going home alone.

Jackson looked around the New Year's Eve party. Typical collection of Chicago dancers and dance whores, friends and hangers-on who either didn't or couldn't make it in the actual world of dance. He'd been invited here by his friend Kurt, who'd recently organized a small avant-garde troupe called the Movement Project. He'd gone to a couple of rehearsals and shows and was impressed by what he saw. Their quick, intricate style of modern dance struck him as ideal for Prosper's skill set.

Prosper. He couldn't stop thinking about her. He even talked to Kurt about her talent, about *Firebird*. He stopped short of asking if Kurt might consider making a place for Prosper in his troupe.

Hell, he didn't even know if Prosper would be interested. They hadn't talked about February, about what was going to happen when he had to leave; in fact, both of them stubbornly avoided the topic. They'd agreed to "no strings attached," but over the weeks they'd spent together, he felt drawn ever closer to her. He wanted to be with her. He wanted more time with her. He wanted to ask her to come to Chicago, not just because he was selfish, but because he truly felt she'd be happier there.

But *Firebird* would open up opportunities at the Townsend she wouldn't want to miss, opportunities she'd worked toward for years. It was a highly respected company, and it was in New York, the capital of the dance world. Why would she choose to leave just to try her hand at a small struggling group like Kurt's? He went back and forth in his mind, weighing the pros and cons of every possibility.

Around him, drunk revelers danced and hung on each other. He felt his shoulder jostled and turned to see a curvaceous blonde woman smiling at him. He knew her, tried to place her.

"Jackson! It's Courtney. Don't you remember me? We danced together at school."

Courtney, Courtney. The only Courtney he remembered had been a skinny, thin-lipped girl who had repulsed him in partnering classes because of the pimples on her back. He looked again. Some plastic surgery on the nose, Restylane in the lips. No more zits.

"Courtney. Hi. Yes, of course I remember you."

"How've you been? You look fantastic! Kurt said you've been in New York."

"Yes. I've been mounting a production of *Firebird* there. New choreography, everything."

"Really?" Her shrill voice and disproportionate lips were squicking him out. She stepped closer, and he stepped back. "Where? Anyplace I'd know?"

"The Townsend Ballet." He turned away and took a drink of his beer. "We start serious rehearsals next week for an opening in February."

"Wow, the Townsend. They have a great reputation."

"They're a small company, but they have good, hardworking dancers. A good director."

"Well, I'm happy for you." She pulled a theatrical pout. "But when are you coming back to Chicago? We need your talents here."

When she said "talents," she put her hand on his lower back. He shifted, and her hand moved lower.

"Oh, I'll be back. I've promised to do some choreography for the Joffrey Ballet." He pulled back a little as her hand moved even lower.

Was she going to squeeze his ass? He turned to face her, but then she used the opportunity to thrust her chest in his face. He looked down, remembered skinny dance-student boobs. More enhancement. They looked like double Ds now.

"Are you still dancing?" he asked.

"Oh, I'm teaching. I got married. Big mistake. Just had a messy divorce. God, it's just horrible out there, the single life. Are you seeing anyone right now?"

Her casual tone didn't hide the desperation behind her voice.

"I am seeing someone. A dancer. For a few weeks now."

"Oh, that's great!" The fake enthusiasm in her voice didn't quite reach her eyes. "Is she at the Townsend?"

"Yeah. She's dancing the Firebird role. Just a coincidence."

"Oh, sure." Courtney winked. "A coincidence. I believe you."

Jackson laughed and shrugged. "Whatever it is, it's a good thing."

"But she must be based in New York. If you're coming back to Chicago—"

"We haven't quite worked that out yet."

"Is she here tonight?"

"No," said Jackson, turning away again. "Work duties. *Nutcracker.*"

"Oh, *Nutcracker.*" Courtney rolled her eyes. "Fun. Well, listen,"— she trailed a perfectly manicured finger down over his bicep—"if you're bored later, after the ball drops, since your dancer isn't in town..."

He frowned. "Thanks. But I'll probably take a pass. I'm in love with her."

He stopped. Where had that come from?

Courtney shrugged, apparently having plumbed the depths of her self-humiliation.

"Good for you. That's great. Well, in that case, a kiss for New Year's." She lunged forward, and he turned his head to catch her pillowy lips on his cheek.

"Okay, happy New Year!" he said. "It was nice to see you again after all these years."

"Sure, Jackson. And really, if you change your mind after the ball drops..."

"I don't think I'll change my mind. I actually think I'm flying back to New York tonight."

Is that really what he was thinking? He must have been, because he put down his beer and headed home to pack. He was going to fly back to New York early, he decided. Because he was in love with Prosper Ware.

CHAPTER FIFTEEN

The Townsend party was in full swing by midnight. New Year's Eve had passed, but the dancers were creating a little New Year's Day cheer of their own. Kristen hosted it, so Prosper expected to be turned away at the door, but Blake arrived just behind her and swept her in on his arm, pulling her toward the kitchen, which was acting as the bar.

"Glad the Ballcracker is over for the season?" he asked with a genuine smile.

"Yeah." She looked around and saw the usual mix of expressions directed back at her. Curiosity, jealousy, hate. One or two people smiled at her. Probably drunk already or not Townsend dancers. The place was wall to wall, hot and loud, with pounding music. Kristen's apartment was large and furnished in bright colors. Some of the dancers were already making out on the huge sofa. She smiled at Blake. "If it wasn't for you, Kristen wouldn't have let me in."

"She asked me the other day to drop you in rehearsals. I think she was only half kidding."

Prosper tried to laugh, but she couldn't. It was a horrible thing for someone to say, and knowing Kristen, she'd meant it. He leaned down to speak next to her ear over the din of the music.

"Don't let them get to you." He squeezed her elbow. "Get something to drink. Enjoy the party. It's hard-core *Firebird* after this, so enjoy your freedom while you can."

She nodded and waved as another partygoer pulled him away.

She turned and went to the kitchen. Kristen gave her a cold smile and nudged the guy next to her, someone Prosper didn't recognize. Her boyfriend? He looked shifty and mean. They made a perfect pair. She changed direction and ran into Glenna. They hugged and exchanged some small talk as best they could in the noisy, crowded space. Since she'd moved in with Jackson, Glenna had remained a faithful friend to her, but they didn't have much to talk about anymore. Prosper thought pretty soon even Glenna would stop trying to be nice. Depressing. She needed a drink. She pushed back into the kitchen and was surprised to see Kristen shoving a beer in her face.

"Drink up, Prosper. It's a party, yeah? Happy New Year!" She hugged Prosper, then backed away. "Have you been losing weight? You look great. Jackson's working you to death, I guess. Wish it was me!" She giggled and clinked her beer with Prosper's. "Drink, drink! Be merry."

Interesting. Drunk enough to be friends with her now, she supposed. Prosper took a swallow of the beer. Ugh, she hated beer, but she choked it down anyway and made her way back out into the living room. Dancers were jumping and grooving to the pounding house music. She moved over to the wall and watched while she nursed her drink. No one moved like ballet dancers. The movement and energy was hypnotic. In fact, she started to feel a little hypnotized. Why was she feeling so woozy? She really had lost weight. She was a lightweight. She hadn't even finished one beer, and she was gone.

No, seriously. She was gone. She clutched at the wall, overcome with dizziness. The faces around her blurred, and the voices grew softer and then louder. She was having trouble even making out who was speaking or where the voices were coming from. She hadn't drunk that much, had she? God, she felt so tired, and her legs wouldn't hold her up. She was going to collapse, and everyone was going to laugh at her, all the weird, unrecognizable people moving through the haze in her brain.

"Hey there." Firm hands took her arms and propped her up, and a face appeared directly in front of her. "Are you okay?"

She squinted through blurred vision. Was it Kristen's friend? She thought she remembered him, but she wasn't sure. "No. I'm not. I need... I need..." She rubbed her face. Her lips weren't working too well either. Her tongue wouldn't form words.

"You need to lie down. Would you like to lie down?"

Prosper nodded gratefully. Yes, she needed to lie down. She was so tired, so drunk. Her legs weren't working. She felt the man lift her up and carry her. So nice. She just needed to rest. He carried her into a room and shut the door. He put her on the bed, and she curled up, relieved and exhausted. There were other people there watching and laughing. They knew she was a lightweight, passing out just a few moments after she arrived...where? Where was she? She couldn't remember where she was, what she was doing here. She thought maybe she was at the hospital again because someone was taking her clothes off.

No, not a hospital. She was at a party. She saw the face of Kristen's friend smiling at her, but it wasn't a nice smile. "It's okay. It's okay," he kept repeating as he tried to ease her dress up. But it wasn't okay. She stood and pushed him away, nearly falling down in the process. She pulled the hem of her dress back down, and then she did stumble. Everyone laughed again, and that made her angry. Furious. Hands grabbed at her, but she hit them back and struggled to the door, pulling at the knob. Locked. *Work the lock, Prosper. How does it work? Turn it.*

Damn. Try the other way.

She concentrated, forced her fingers to move. She had it now. It was unlocked. She turned the knob, but Kristen's friend tried again to pull her away. She turned and did the only thing she remembered to do in a situation like this. She brought her knee up with all her strength between his legs.

A groan, curse words, more laughter. Why wouldn't they help her instead of standing around laughing? She turned back to the door, got it open, and lurched outside. It slammed behind her, locking again. Jesus, as if she'd go back in there. She leaned on the wall. The room was spinning. Good God, she was wasted. She looked up into a familiar face. What the hell was his name?

He was talking to her, but she couldn't understand him. The music pounded in her ears. He seemed to be asking her questions. He was pointing at her legs, and Prosper looked down. God, where were her shoes and tights? She looked back up at him in confusion. He pushed past her and pounded on the door.

Oh, Blake. Blake was his name. He would get her tights for her. Her shoes, at least. It was way too cold to go barefoot. No way would she be able to put her tights on, though. She was too tired. Someone else would have to help her put her tights on.

Strong arms came around her, cradled her. Jackson was here for her at last. Jackson would help her. She buried her face in his neck and sighed in relief, breathed in the scent of him.

No, not Jackson. Blake.

God, she was fucked-up. She needed to go to bed.

Jackson got home just before noon. Prosper didn't greet him; the house was quiet. He'd planned to surprise her, but she wasn't here to be surprised. Out to lunch with a friend? No, her bag was on the counter. Still asleep? He knew she'd gone to a party the night before. He smiled and headed to the bedroom to wake her.

He pushed open the door. What he saw made his blood turn cold and his voice rise in a roar.

"What the fuck is going on here?"

Prosper was asleep in his bed, and Blake was sprawled out beside her on top of the covers. At the sound of Jackson's voice, he shot up, rubbing his eyes. Prosper jumped too, coming awake with a start. She took one bleary-eyed look at Jackson and ran to the bathroom with a hand pressed to her mouth.

Blake rolled off the other side of the bed, holding his arms out. "It's not what it looks like."

"It better not fucking be what it looks like, because it looks like you were sleeping with Prosper in my fucking bed!"

"Something happened at the party last night."

Jackson could hear the sound of Prosper being sick. He yelled at Blake on his way to the bathroom. "What? What happened at the party?"

"Prosper got sick. Someone drugged her. When I found her, she was half-undressed, but I don't think they actually did anything—"

"You don't think who did anything? What the fuck are you talking about?" He checked on Prosper, who was standing at the sink now, holding her head. God, she looked terrible. He tilted her head back and made her look at him, checking for color and alertness. She was alert but definitely green.

"Are you going to be sick again?"

"If you don't let me lie back down, then probably yes."

He wet a washcloth and slapped it on her forehead, then helped her back to the bed, where she curled up under the covers with a groan. He turned to Blake, who was still standing on the other side of the bed, and put his hands on his hips.

"Explain. All of it."

"Look, I don't exactly know—"

"Explain everything, or I will beat you senseless."

"Okay. I saw Prosper at the party. She was fine. About fifteen minutes later I saw her again, and she was nearly passed out, half-undressed—"

"Half-undressed? By who?"

"I'm pretty sure it was some guys Kristen invited."

"Some guys?"

"Look, calm down. Nothing happened; I'm sure of it. I checked."

"You checked?" Jackson felt his blood pounding in his ears. "You checked her?"

"I checked with the guys in the room. She never actually passed out. They didn't do anything. I think she kicked one of them in the crotch. He was pretty pissed about it. Nothing else happened, okay? I brought her back here, and then I was worried about leaving her alone with the drugs in her system, so I stayed. That's it, the whole story. I didn't want her dying in her sleep or something."

"Why didn't you take her to the hospital?"

"She said she didn't want to go."

"No hospital," Prosper moaned, not even opening her eyes. "I just want to sleep."

Jackson knelt beside the bed. "Prosper. Honey." He stroked her cheek until her eyes cracked open and she focused on him. "What happened to you at the party? Do you remember?"

"Somebody...somebody took my shoes. Kristen's friend."

"Just took your shoes? That's all he did?"

"He took my tights too. I kicked him in the nuts."

"I told you," said Blake. "They insisted nothing else happened. I chewed them out, and we left."

"They insisted, and you just believed them? They drugged her! Did you call the police?"

"No police," Prosper said in a weak voice from the bed.

Blake sighed. "I didn't go to the police because—"

Jackson spun on Blake. "Because it was your fucking friends! You didn't want to get them in trouble! That bitch Kristen—"

"They weren't my friends! It was some guys Kristen knew."

"Somebody needs to pay for this!"

"At Prosper's expense?"

Prosper clutched her head and groaned. Blake lowered his voice.

"You're angry," Blake said. "Yeah, I'm angry too. But parading her to the hospital and making her fill out police reports is the last thing she's going to want to do."

Jackson scowled at him. "And you just accept this? Dancers drugging other dancers, setting them up to be raped out of spite over a fucking part?"

"You don't understand, in a small company like this, just how vicious the politics can be."

"Politics? This isn't politics. This is sociopathy!"

"Don't yell at me, Jackson. Yeah, they drugged her. It was shitty and small-minded, and yeah, she almost got seriously hurt. I had no idea, and I sure as hell wasn't in on it. I just wanted to get her someplace safe. And this is at least partly your fault! It's your fault everyone hates her. And her health is shit. I can't even partner her anymore without feeling like I'm going to break her. What the hell have you been doing to her? You're wearing her down—"

"I haven't even been in town." No, he hadn't been in town. He'd left her alone, left her to defend herself from the selfish narcissists who surrounded her. He pointed at Blake.

"You're going to tell Lawrence. You're going to go to him and tell him everything that happened—"

"Jackson—"

"I don't care if it gets your bitch girlfriend in trouble—"

"Jackson! Listen. I already did. I already called and told him what went on at the party. He's going to ask Kristen to leave. She was going to leave anyway."

Jackson stood and seethed. He wanted to throw in the towel on the whole thing—*Firebird*, the Townsend, all of it. He didn't want Prosper to set one toe onstage with dancers who would even conceive of such evil plans. He looked over at her pallid face, her thin frame. Blake was right. She looked like death warmed over. Either he was going crazy, or she'd dropped five more pounds in the short time he'd been gone.

He looked back at Blake, mastering his temper. "Okay. I appreciate you getting her home and keeping an eye on her."

"No problem. And I really didn't have anything to do with it. I swear. You know I wouldn't—There's no way I could have—"

"Yeah, Blake. I know."

Another moan from Prosper. "I'm thirsty again."

"I'd better be going," said Blake. Jackson showed him to the door on his way to get a bottle of water for Prosper. Blake took his arm before he left.

"Look, Jackson. You've got to let her go. I know you care about her, man, but you've made a world of trouble for her casting her in your ballet. She's a wreck. She's not star material; she's just not. She has what it takes here"—he pointed to his feet—"but she doesn't have it here." He pointed to his head. "You should have left her back in the corps. I'm saying that as Prosper's friend. And you know what else?" He looked at Jackson with reproach. "You should have kept your dick in your pants."

"Nice speech," said Jackson. He listened to Blake's words, and some part of him knew Blake was right. But another part of him thought that if Blake didn't stop talking, he'd choke the life out of him with his bare, shaking hands.

"Jackson..." came Prosper's weak voice from the bedroom.

"See you, Blake," said Jackson, shutting the door in his face.

16   Chapter Sixteen

Jackson took the water up to Prosper and propped her in his arms so she could drink it. She was so thin, so unhealthy. Blake was right. Taking her to the hospital, making her press charges against Kristen and her cronies, all of it would have made her suffer, and she'd suffered enough.

She'd suffered enough at his hands. When she fell asleep again and he was sure she wouldn't fight him, he carried her upstairs to the other room. When she began to stir again, he brought her milk and crackers. She refused the milk, and he offered water. When she refused that too, Jackson knelt beside her and took her chin in his hands.

"You are sick. If you do not at least drink something, we'll leave for the hospital in five minutes."

"No. No hospital!"

"Then drink." He held the milk to her lips, and when he was satisfied she'd had enough for the moment, he put it down on the side table. She seemed a little better. She was more alert, and her skin tone wasn't so green. He took a deep breath. "Prosper, honey. Tell me what you remember about last night."

"I don't really remember anything. It's hazy. Blake said they drugged me. I guess they wanted to rape me, but I was a little too pissed off for that."

"Pissed off?"

"That I couldn't hold my alcohol. I thought I was drunk. I know I kicked one guy in the nuts."

"Yes, we already went over that. And I'm glad you did. He deserved it." Jackson sighed. The look on her face killed him. He would have given anything to make it go away.

"They really do hate me."

"Some of them hate you. Their problem. Not yours. I think it was Kristen's attempt to send you running. We should go to the police, press charges."

Prosper was already shaking her head. "No police. I just want— If they hate me that much—"

"No. You're not quitting. Don't even think about it. I thought the same thing, but if you do that, they win. No fucking way. No."

"I'm supposed to go to work tomorrow and face them all?"

"Kristen will be gone. I talked to Lawrence while you were sleeping. Her contract with Townsend has already been terminated. But you're not quitting. We're going to turn this around, and we're going to get you healthy again. Look at you. You look anorexic. Jesus Christ, Prosper."

She turned away. "I've been too nervous to eat. And too busy. I've missed you." Her eyes were tearing up. "Jackson, I can't...I can't..."

He ran soft fingertips across her cheek, wiped her tears away.

"I can't survive without you," she said. "I really don't think I can."

He gathered her up and squeezed her. "I know how you feel."

"When you leave, when you go back to Chicago... God... Jackson... I don't know what I'm going to do."

He buried his face in her hair and rocked her. "I'm not leaving you again, okay? We'll figure something out. But I can't leave you. Do you know why?" He turned her face up and looked down at his Firebird. "Listen to me. Do you know why I won't leave you? Because I love you, you crazy, messed-up girl. I love you so much."

She sniffled, her wide green eyes hopeful and terrified at once. "You love me? You really do?"

"How could you doubt it? I'm not letting you go. Not now." He twisted her hair in his hand, held her head against his chest. She was still shuddery and scared. He was too, for that matter, but at least finally she knew the truth.

"I love you too, Jackson. I've wanted to tell you for the longest time. I know that wasn't the deal."

He laughed. "The deal? Deals change. And there's a new deal now. You stay in this room until you're healthy again. Your body is my instrument. I want you to feed it and care for it. If you won't do it for you, you'll do it for me. If you lose one more pound, I'll beat you black-and-blue. Do you understand me?"

She nodded with a smile. "Yes, Sir."

"And we don't play until your weight improves. You don't come sleep in my bed again until you're strong enough to survive what I want to do to you right now."

Her eyes opened wide, pleading.

"I mean it. You're to gain weight and get stronger first. If you want me, that's what you have to do. Now eat some of these crackers. The milk too."

She sighed, but she took the plate and glass from his hands. "Yes, Sir."

Jackson stuck to his word, although it was painful. He wanted nothing more on earth than to touch her, take her. Beat her, lick her, sink between her legs. But he didn't do any of that. He let her recuperate, and two days later, when they returned to the Townsend, she held her head high.

As he suspected, most of the dancers were sympathetic, their jealousy replaced by outrage at what Kristen had done. Whispers about Kristen's sudden parting were replaced by relief that she was gone. The void left by the departure of her negative energy was filled with excitement for the spring season to come. Kristen was replaced by Lynette, a talented soloist who was overjoyed to be promoted to the Tsarina role.

So going full steam into *Firebird* rehearsals, the company felt a sense of optimistic solidarity. The dancers worked together like a well-oiled machine. Blake and Prosper seemed to find a new closeness, a greater connection. And Jackson, secure in his feelings for her, felt no jealousy at all.

But Prosper still worried. To Jackson's chagrin, she still fell victim to fits of panic and insecurity. The difficult lift, where Blake sent her airborne, still didn't meet Jackson's approval because she was too fearful to do it right.

"You're turning in! Try again."

Blake nodded. "You're turning in, Prosper. I'm more likely to drop you that way. Just trust me."

"I do trust you," she said, stalking back across the floor to get back in position.

"You're a Firebird," said Jackson. "You're supposed to be on fucking fire. No fear!"

She spun on him. "No fear? What is that? I don't understand that as it pertains to this lift!"

"No fear. Come on, Prosper. You can do this. Just stop stressing so much and fucking do it. It's your self-doubt, it's your own mind that stops you."

"I know that! God!" She ran from the room. Blake glared at him.

"Smooth. Nice pep talk."

"I don't see you trying to shore up her confidence."

"I told you, she doesn't have any. Everything she does comes from a place of fear." Blake snorted and turned to stretch against the barre, but Jackson froze still.

Everything she does comes from a place of fear.

It was true. Why hadn't he ever pieced it together before? Fear of failure, fear of displeasing him. Fear of not being good enough. Blake, with the strange connection dance partners developed, had understood it. Somehow Jackson had not.

"That's it for today," he said to Blake. He went in search of Prosper and found her in the back of the costume closet, hiding behind a mountain of tulle.

"Prosper, honey."

The tulle shifted, sniffled. Revealed a shock of tousled orange waves. She'd pulled down her bun so she could hide her tearful face behind the curtain of her hair.

"Come here." He got down on the floor beside her and pushed away the pile of costumes. "I want to talk to you."

"I don't want to talk. I want to be alone."

"Maybe so, but we're going to talk. I want you to tell me."

She drew a hand across her cheek, smeared tears across tiny freckles. "Tell you what?"

"Tell me what you're hiding. Tell me why you're so afraid."

"I'm just... That lift..."

"No." He took her hand, made her focus. "This isn't about the lift. This is about why Prosper is so afraid. Why Prosper has to be perfect. Why Prosper can never be happy with herself."

He tried to make her look at him, but she pulled away with a fresh torrent of tears, burying her face in the pile of skirts beside her.

"Prosper, baby. Talk to me."

"I can't."

"I need to know." He pulled her away from the skirts and encircled her in a tight grasp. "Talk to me. Let me help you. Please! I love you. And I'm warning you, we're not leaving this pile of tulle until you open up to me."

Her sobs were broken by a soft giggle.

"That's right. This tulle is itchy, and it probably hasn't been washed since *Nutcracker* ended. It smells weird too. Now talk."

She buried her face in his side. She was quiet a long moment, but then she finally spoke in a quavery voice.

"I killed someone."

Jackson froze. Not what he'd expected. "You what?"

She started to cry again. "I killed my baby sister."

Jackson rubbed her back, slow and steady, considering what to say. "Tell me what happened."

"My mother was upstairs. She was sleeping. She'd been up late with my stepfather fighting. I was playing with my dolls, and I didn't see my sister open the door. She had just turned two. I didn't see her leave!"

She shivered against him. Jackson pulled her closer and stroked her hair. "I'm sure you didn't."

"If I had seen her, I would have told my mother, but I wasn't paying attention. I was playing wedding with my dolls. Barbie and Ken were getting married." She sniffled. "My sister crossed the street and wandered into a retention pond. She drowned. They looked for her everywhere, and they finally found her there in the water. And my mother..."

Something inside Jackson shuddered. "She said it was your fault."

"If I had been paying attention, if I had been watching her... If I had only seen her—I was so caught up in myself!"

Jackson frowned against her hair, aghast at the horrible implication that she had been at fault. "How old were you, Prosper?"

"I was four. I was old enough."

"Old enough to parent a two-year-old?"

"I was almost five!"

"Your mother blamed you because she couldn't blame herself." Jackson's heart clenched as he thought of Prosper as an innocent four-year-old, blamed for her mother's awful mistake. "Prosper, your mother was responsible for your sister, not you. You were only a child yourself. She only blamed you because she couldn't deal with her own guilt."

"But the truth is, I..." Her face crumpled into more guilty tears as she looked up at him. She looked like a child herself, the terrified four-year-old she must have been. "I was jealous of my sister. I dreamed about her getting lost so it could be just me and my mother again. I wanted my mom all to myself. I didn't want her to be married to my stepdad. I didn't want her to have his child and love her more than me. I hated my baby sister. So when she drowned, when my mother said it was my fault, I really did believe it was my fault. That somehow I had wanted her to drown." She buried her face in her hands and sobbed.

"Oh, honey." He stared at the bowed head before him, the bright red hair that had marked her as an error in judgment from birth. Not her error, but her mother and father's. He thought of her as a four-year-old, the weight of guilt she'd shouldered over an innocuous mistake, and the penance of perfection she'd carried for twenty years since then. He took her in his arms and rocked her, wishing he could take it all away. Wishing he could beat her mother senseless for what she'd done. "Prosper," he said in her ear, "you can't take the blame for what happened to your sister. It was a terrible mistake, but it wasn't your mistake. Your mother should have been watching her."

"But what if I make another big mistake?" she sobbed. "What if something terrible happens?"

"So to prevent that, you spend every waking moment trying to be perfect? Don't you see how silly that is? Life happens. Accidents happen no matter how hard you try. But you don't have to be perfect for me to love you. Mistakes are part of life. Nobody's perfect. Nobody should try to be. It can't be that important to you. It shouldn't be."

"I want to be perfect for you!"

"Movements, steps can be perfect. People can't."

"I can be. If I try. I want to be perfect for you. I want you to love me! If you ever stopped loving me—"

He put a finger to her lips. "I love you as you are, Prosper. My love is not conditional."

He watched her. Her hands were in little fists against his chest. Her lips trembled, and her eyes were shimmery with tears. He wiped at her damp cheeks.

"Do you think I'll stop loving you? Really? If you make an innocent mistake?"

He felt her body shake against his. All those tears. How many tears had she stored up inside?

"You know what?" he said. "You can slaughter my ballet at the premiere. You can fall off pointe and miss every turn. You can kick Blake in the nuts during every single fucking passé, and I'll still love you. I will. You could never make enough mistakes to make me love you less. Never."

She was quiet a moment, then whispered into the hollow of his shoulder, "What if I turn in on that lift?"

"Well then, I'll fucking kill you. I swear to God I will." Her soft giggle made some hard knot of worry inside him thaw. She would be all right. Now that he knew what haunted her, knew why she drove herself so hard, he could start to reverse the damage her mother had done.

"Beautiful girl," he said against her ear, "you're more to me than some fucking ballet. Don't you know that?"

She made a soft noise of assent against his chest.

"No. Say it to me. Out loud. I'm more to you than some fucking ballet."

"I'm more to you than some fucking ballet."

"Like you mean it."

"I'm more to you than some fucking ballet!" she repeated, giggling.

"Damn skippy. Now let's crawl out of this tulle hole. You hit the showers, and we'll go home. I think it's high time you moved back into my room."

The walk home seemed interminable to Prosper. It had been weeks since he'd made love to her. He hadn't even spanked her, although she'd done everything in her power to provoke him before giving up.

"I'll spank you when I'm damn ready to," he'd told her. "And I'll do a whole lot more than that too. Now eat your dinner." He'd checked her weight to make sure it was going up and forced her back to healthy habits. She slept better. She felt healthier now, stronger.

And now that she'd told him her terrible guilty secret, she felt healthier mentally as well. She couldn't live in fear of accidents. She had to appreciate what she had. She had to live her life and not be afraid of not being perfect.

As they neared the house, Jackson squeezed her hand and looked down at her.

"What are you thinking about?" he asked with a smile. "Naughty thoughts?"

"Yes. And about how much I love you. How lucky I am."

"How lucky we are."

He led her inside and straight up to the bedroom. He was silent as he stripped off her clothes. He touched her all over, his big hands stroking, holding, pinching, brushing over her skin. She shivered, cold and hot at once. He twisted his hands in her hair and kissed her forehead.

"Undress me."

Prosper pulled off his shirt. She had to touch, desperately wanted to touch. She moved forward, ran her fingers up and down the smooth ridges that defined his midsection. She traced his shoulders and went up on her toes to kiss the birthmark just below his neck. He drew in his breath, his fingers skimming the sides of her hips, then pushed her back. "Focus. What did I tell you to do?"

Prosper sighed and reached for his belt. Her fingers shook as she worked the metal buckle. His faded jeans revealed the outline of his erection underneath. She bit her lip to keep herself from moaning and embarrassing herself as she knelt to undo his button and draw down his zipper. She pulled the jeans down over his hips until he stood in only his boxer briefs. Her breath left in a rush.

"While you're down there, girl..."

She peeled down the boxers and pressed her lips to his warm, rigid cock. Her eyes closed, and she thought again how much she loved him as she dropped kisses along the length of his thick shaft. Her tongue flicked out and probed the hole at the tip of his cock, savoring the drop of precum there. He pushed her back with an indrawn breath.

"A condom. Hurry."

She went for the rubber and then dropped to her knees before him, rolling it on. She caressed his hard length over the latex for just a moment before he pushed her hands away and thrust between her lips. His hard length filled her mouth and throat. She clutched at his thighs and pulled him closer. She could feel his legs trembling as she sucked and worshipped his cock. When he drew away, she couldn't stifle her cry of disappointment.

He pulled her up and half walked, half carried her to the bed. He bent her over, twisting her hair hard in his hands until she cried out from the pain. She arched back for him, wanting him closer. He parted her thighs roughly with his knees.

"Open wide. Wider!"

She spread her legs as wide as she could. His dick nudged her opening, and she jumped, the contact burning her with arousal like fire. Her legs shook from the effort of control, from the effort of not pushing herself backward and impaling herself on his cock.

"Wait, girl." The low warning made her whimper.

"Please. Oh, Sir, please..." Then she gasped as he pressed to her and eased inside, inch by inch. Oh God. She wanted him to possess her, to fuck her. She clutched at the comforter, overcome with lust and desire. His hands kneaded her hips as he paused, seated to the hilt inside her.

He groaned and withdrew, then plunged forward again. He began fucking her hard and fast. Her breasts bounced against the bed, and she felt wild, lost. She reached back for him, and he drew her arms behind her, holding them hard in his strong fingers. He slowed, moved in and out of her in a teasing rhythm, hard, fast, slow, deep. Her clit pulsed, and her hips bucked for contact whenever he withdrew from her. He drove her mad, drove her arousal higher and higher until her body was no longer hers but his. She belonged to him, and he controlled everything she felt, every erotic ache and throb. They fit together perfectly. Her shoulders tensed; her back arched further. She ground her clit against the bed, reveling in the delicious build of arousal, the inexorable approach to climax, a climax controlled not by her but by him.

"Please, Sir! Please let me come."

He leaned over her, his breath in her hair. "You want to come, girl?"

"Yes," she begged. "Please, yes!"

"And who makes you come? Who do you belong to?"

"You! I belong to you!"

"I love you, Prosper," he whispered just before he bit down on her earlobe. "Come for me."

He drove into her harder, drove her against the bed so she felt captured. Something inside her broke loose and overran its bounds. Gushing, hot, uncontrollable pleasure. Unbelievable, bountiful riches filling her, satisfying her. Love like an avalanche. *Prosperity.* When her orgasm finally left her, he stayed inside her, connected to her. She cried—not from fear, at last, but from joy.

CHAPTER SEVENTEEN

It was the night before the *Firebird* premiere. Prosper thought the final run-through had gone exceedingly well. Lawrence had clapped Jackson on the back and issued prolific praise before turning to Prosper and hugging her.

"I knew you could do it all along!"

It really was a stunning production. The set was gorgeous, Kostchei's garden rendered in rich colors. The whimsical, bizarre costumes were spectacular, and the dancers in them were fully invested in making the groundbreaking production a success. When Prosper put on her costume, tears welled in her eyes. She looked in the mirror and felt herself become the Firebird. It was inside her now, the fire, the ability. She thought she could take on the entire world, wave her red-orange tail feathers, and set any catastrophe back to rights.

After the run-through, Jackson had taken her to dinner. She'd smiled and laughed with him until her jaws ached. He was bursting with excitement and well-deserved pride. They talked about *Firebird* and then about Chicago. Prosper had been invited to join the company of Jackson's friend Kurt.

They had taken a weekend trip to meet the other dancers and tour the small facility. Prosper felt immediately at home. The dancers were friendly and enthusiastic, and there were no principals, no soloists, no corps. Every dancer was just a dancer. They all participated and contributed according to their abilities and strengths. Some of them were involved in choreography and even costuming and production design. They were all full of pride for what they'd built. Because of that, their company was finding success and expanding. Prosper was overjoyed when they extended the invitation for her to join. There would be a learning curve, but she knew she could do it. Jackson assured her she was going to knock them dead.

But better than that, better than joining this new, exciting company, Prosper was going to be in Chicago with Jackson. *No strings attached* had, at some point, changed into *you're coming with me.* She would have followed him anywhere, even to Kostchei's evil kingdom. To follow him to the thriving dance world of Chicago was icing on the cake.

She would dance *Firebird* until mid-April, and then she and Jackson were going to leave New York. She was actually relieved to be rid of the big city. Jackson had questioned her for a long time to be sure she really felt that way. The truth was, she'd never been comfortable in New York. She was looking forward to meeting Jackson's family and friends and setting up a home with him. She was looking forward to life in his arms.

After dinner Jackson took her home, still brimming with energy. She could tell from the look in his eyes that something fun was coming. He took her upstairs and told her to strip and wait for him. He returned a few moments later with a wardrobe bag. He opened it, and Prosper gasped.

"Jackson! You will get in so much trouble. Oh my God!"

He held her Firebird costume in his hands. Its gaudy, showy sequins, rubies, and feathers looked wildly out of place in Jackson's white bedroom, a shocking explosion of color. The strange juxtaposition of stage and home unbalanced her. Prosper shook her head, half-scandalized, half-awestruck.

"I can't believe you took it. Maureen will kill you."

"Maureen will never know." He grinned at her. "Put it on."

Prosper laughed, feeling daring and naughty. While she pulled it on, Jackson stripped.

"Go. Put your hands on the wall," he told her.

She felt shivery with excitement. Blood thrummed in her veins. Jackson rooted through his drawer of implements and came up with a bright red riding crop. She'd never seen that before! She turned back to the wall, hyperaware of every sensation: the itchiness of the costume against her bare skin, the soft tickling of the feathers that lined her tutu. My God, she was going to cream all over the gusset, and Maureen would know what a slut she was. She looked back over her shoulder to see Jackson smiling at her.

"I've got you. A Firebird, trapped right here in my house."

She giggled. "You've had me for a long time now, and you know it."

"Mouthy little critter." He snapped the back of her thigh with the crop. She squeaked and shifted from foot to foot.

"Nipples against the wall. Knees too."

She pressed herself forward with a moan. The metallic thread inside the cups of the bodice scratched her sensitive nipples. She looked back at Jackson.

"You'll get in so much trouble if this gets damaged," she said.

"No. You will. Because I'll blame it on you."

"I'm serious, Jackson! You know how Maureen is about the costumes. At least...at least..." She eyed his bulging erection and swallowed. "Just please don't get any cum on it."

"Hush, little bird. Enough chirping." The next flick of the crop caught her under her left ass cheek and left a strip of hot fire. He tapped her ass with it and pulled her away from the wall.

"Bend over. Grab your ankles."

She did as he asked, folding her body over carefully, cringing when the costume pulled tight between her legs, wedging into her pussy. She felt the feathers in the front tickling her shins while the feathers in the back must have been sticking straight up in the air. He delivered a few more swishing strokes, hitting her on the outside of her ass cheeks and the insides of her thighs. She knew he would be careful not to mark her. Well, not too badly, anyway.

"Ouch. Ouch!" She gritted her teeth and held her ankles hard. "Owww...*oh*!" Each smack was sharp, liquid pain spreading out from the point of contact. Her clit ached and throbbed more and more the longer he went on. God, Maureen would kill her for the mess she was making of the costume's nylon panties...but oh...*ohhhhh*...

"Hm," Jackson said. "You look kind of like a turkey with your feathers sticking up like that in the back." Prosper giggled. He came closer, stood behind her, and poked her through the material of the gusset with his erection. "Or maybe a peacock."

His randy prodding was about to push her off balance. "I thought only males had the fancy feathers."

"Silence, turkey girl," he said with another slice of the crop against her outer thigh. She yelped and finally lost her balance. They went down in a tumble of stiff tulle, rhinestones, and feathers. They laughed and then both noticed at the same time the lone red-orange feather wafting down to the floor.

"You are so dead," Prosper whispered.

Jackson turned over on top of her and pressed his cock against the material at her opening. "I'm going to cut this part off," he said, pulling at the stretchy fabric covering her swollen pussy.

Prosper gasped. "No. Don't you dare!"

"'No?' What is this word 'no' I hear on my submissive's lips? I have to open it up somehow, or I won't be able to fuck you."

"Jackson, please." Her voice rose to a panicked squeal as he twisted the material in his fingers.

"Isn't there another costume? A backup?"

"No, there's not!"

"Well, that's unfortunate."

Prosper prayed he was teasing. There was nothing more terrifying to a dancer than a damaged costume.

"Okay, girl," he finally said. "Let's get this off you."

She breathed a sigh of relief as he eased the ornate garment off her shoulders and down over her hips. When he finished and tossed it aside, she gazed at him in entreaty.

"Please, Sir, may I hang it up?"

"No, girl, you may not," he answered, nibbling at her lips. "Now fly over there and fetch me a condom."

She stood and walked to the bedside table. On the way back she eyed the crumpled costume on the floor.

"No." At the warning in his voice, she squelched the urge to defy him, and let him pull her back down. As he opened the cellophane and rolled the condom on, he watched her, bemused. "I bet I can make you forget that costume lying there." He drew one of her nipples into his mouth and rolled it between his teeth before grazing it softly. She cried out and reached for him. "Yes. Pretty sure I can."

His fingers made slow, maddening circles around her clit, not quite touching it. She arched against him, shivering at the teasing torture. "Ohhhh...oh..."

"Yes," he murmured against her lips as she closed her eyes and tried to hang on to her sanity. "I think I can make you forget."

But she'd already forgotten, her mind focused only on his blazing blue eyes, his agile fingers, and the hard cock nudging her pussy lips. She bucked her hips against him, tensing her thighs.

"Please!"

"No, not yet." He reached over for the costume and wrapped one of the clear elastic shoulder straps around her wrists. He used the other stretchy strap to tether her to the foot of the bed frame.

"No," she whispered.

"Yes. You keep those hands still. If you break either of those straps, Maureen will take off your head."

He picked up the feather beside her. He teased the skin of her stomach, her hips. She felt deep relief that after years of being pawed and hauled around by partners, she wasn't ticklish in the least. This she could endure easily. He teased the inside of her arms, then tickled it down across the tops of her thigh. She smiled at him. He smiled back, a devilish grin, and then spread her legs and lowered his lips to her clit. *Oh my God. No.* Tickling she could endure. But not this. She clenched her arm muscles with the effort it took not to pull, not to flail in her bonds. He ignored her predicament, focused instead on kissing her clit. He drew his tongue against it in soft, erratic touches that were—purposely, she knew—not quite enough. All the wet, warm caresses did was ramp her arousal up another level, from flaring to burning. *Still, be still. The costume!*

He reached up and flicked her nipples while he teased her pussy with his mouth. Next level: conflagration. God, she was so hot and wet for him. Her pussy ached to be filled, an ache that grew to an almost unbearable urge. Her arms trembled from the strain of holding still. Her thighs tensed, and her legs kicked, but he gave her no relief. Finally, when she was out of her mind from the hot, teasing pleasure he gave her, he rose over her and released her hands.

She found herself suddenly free but still captured. Her arms locked around him as he impaled her with his cock. She held on to him, breathing in his scent, totally filled by him. The pleasure in her center built, thickened. The intensity was unbearable. His thrusts were urgent, touching the deepest part of her.

"Come now." He held her tight, and her hands flew out, scrabbled for purchase as the orgasm ripped through her. She felt Jackson come with her, driving into her hard, and she gave herself up to his power. She was vaguely aware of soft velvet and cool rhinestones against her palm. When she returned to her senses, she looked up to find Jackson watching her thoughtfully, twirling the red-orange feather in his hand.

EPILOGUE

Prosper stood backstage with Blake, but her mind was on Jackson. He was in the audience. She missed him, but she was okay without him. She felt he was right there with her anyway—in the steps her body had memorized, in the fanciful costume that adorned her, sans one feather. Maureen hadn't noticed, luckily. The feather was safe at home in Jackson's chest of equipment. A gift from the Firebird to the couple she'd brought together with her magical grace.

Prosper was excited. The moment had finally arrived. It was time to bring Jackson's vision to life, show his creation to the curious audience who rustled playbills and seat cushions beyond the heavy velvet curtains.

"Nervous?" Blake whispered. His hand reached for hers.

"No, not at all. I'm fine."

"Don't turn in—"

"On the lift. I know. Believe me. I won't."

Blake laughed. They both stretched, and Prosper flexed her toes. She heard the quiet strains of the introduction begin and watched the curtains for the moment they would slide open. She listened for the musical cue to fly onto the stage and inhabit the role Jackson had choreographed for her. She would do it perfectly for him. Well, as perfectly as she could.

The curtain opened, and the lights blinded her, filling her with the familiar impetus to soar, to perform. The ballet unfolded, lovely and lyrical. She performed for the audience, of course, but more importantly, she performed for him. Every *port de bras* was an embrace for him, every *glissade* or *pirouette* a love song from her heart.

And when the lift came, she ran to her partner without fear or hesitation holding her back. She felt herself buoyed by hope, soaring with happiness.

Like magic, she flew.

 The End

If you enjoyed *Firebird*, check out Annabel Joseph's BDSM Ballet series: *Waking Kiss* and *Fever Dream*.

Waking Kiss, the first in a duo of gripping love stories...

A stranger in the wings, a traitorous pair of toe shoes, and a traumatic turn dancing with The Great Rubio... For ballerina Ashleigh Keaton, it's been one hell of a night.

But it's not over yet. When Rubio drags her to a private party at his friend's house in the ritzy part of London, she meets Liam Wilder, a lifestyle dominant and frighteningly seductive man. Liam pursues Ashleigh, attracted by her strength and talent, but she has secrets— an abusive past and a crippling fear of intimacy that prevents her from connecting to anyone, especially a playboy reputed to be legendary in bed.

Eventually he wins her trust and sets out to heal the troubled dancer, awakening her to a world of sensual abandon in a series of BDSM "sessions" at his home. But how pure are his motives? Is he helping her or endangering her fragile soul? Liam hides his own destructive secrets, and so does Fernando Rubio, their temperamental friend. Over time the three become embroiled in a tangle of artifice, fears, and lies that threaten to undo everything they've worked for.

Will Ashleigh and Liam find the strength to defeat their demons? Or are they cursed to sleepwalk through life forever, afraid to experience the passion and intimacy of love?

Turn the page to read an excerpt...

ANNABEL JOSEPH

An excerpt from *Waking Kiss*

I kept my head down all the way home, not wanting to draw anyone's attention. I sought solace in invisibility like I always did. About halfway there it started to rain, making big dots on my heather-gray hoodie and tee shirt. The sky darkened and a full storm swept in, complete with lightning and thunder. I stalked on, letting the rain soak me while everyone around me ducked into shops and under awnings. By the time I got to my building I was drenched down to my bra and panties. My hair plastered in wet streaks across my face as a freak gust of wind propelled me through the building door and into the cement stairwell that led to my apartment.

"Fuck you," I muttered as the door crashed closed behind me. How dare the wind slam the door on me? It felt like another insult, not as bad as Rubio ignoring me, but close. I pushed the hair back from my eyes, shouldered my dance bag, and started up the stairs to the third floor. I turned the corner and was digging for my keys when the shape of a man moved out from the shadows.

"Oh my God!" I wasn't sure if I screamed it or mouthed it. My heart kicked into overdrive and my hands came out to ward off the intruder. It took a few seconds to process the fact that the intruder was Liam, looking taller and more imposing than ever in the claustrophobic hallway of my low-rent building.

"What are you doing here?" I asked. My breath huffed out in a gasp. "How did you know this was my place?"

He blinked, staring at the front of my soaked hoodie. "My driver has an excellent memory."

Oh yes, the silent, uniformed driver. He'd walked me right to this door, and it hadn't occurred to me that in his insistence to do so, Liam would know where I lived.

"You're soaked," he said, taking a step closer. He was in jeans, the expensive, weathered kind that cling to a man's body in all the right places. He'd paired them with a sage pullover and an equally weathered, caramel-colored leather jacket that probably cost two months of my dancer's salary. He was completely dry.

I clutched my sodden bag closer to my side. "Why aren't you wet? How long have you been here?"

"Not long. I would have called but I didn't have your number. I wanted to bring you this." He held out a single rose. "It's from last night's performance, to replace the one Rubio...ate."

I stared at it, awed by his thoughtfulness. The rose was velvety pale pink, just like the other one. "Where did you get it? I mean, how—"

"The flowers were still in the back, in a box. Yves was very helpful."

"You know Yves?"

"I know Yves." He frowned. "And Ruby too, although it pains me sometimes to call him a friend."

I took the flower and held it to my nose, swallowing back emotion as I stared at him. He'd gone to the theater to find a replacement rose for me. It was the nicest thing anyone had done for me in months. "Thank you," I said. "I felt bad about the other one."

"I know. I felt bad about a lot of things that happened yesterday. I made Ruby apologize to you, but I should have apologized too." He ran a hand through his hair and looked at the floor, then back at me. "I should have listened when you said you weren't a party person. I should have read your signals better. I should have seen you home myself after I kicked Ruby out. I should have done a lot of things I didn't do. I guess my main concern is whether you're okay."

It was my turn to talk. To say I was perfectly fine, that it was no big deal. I wanted to say all the right words but they wouldn't come. I could feel my face breaking. I didn't want to start bawling in front of him—I was so ugly when I cried. No graceful, pretty tears here. More like awful, miserable, emotional-weirdo tears, so it was really, really important that I get away from him. I clutched the rose to my chest and searched for my keys.

"Ashleigh."

"What?" My voice sounded thick and weird. Maybe he wouldn't notice since he didn't know me that well. And why the fuck were keys as elusive as unicorns when you needed to find them in your purse? I saw him reach out in my peripheral vision, and then he took my face in one of his hands, just gripped it between thumb and fingers. Our gazes met and locked. His eyes were liquid amber, even more beautiful than I remembered. He came close, so close to me, and I realized he was going to kiss me. He tilted my face and brushed his lips across mine with the barest hint of pressure.

It wasn't a lucid decision—*okay, I'm going to cry now*—but as his lips moved over mine, the tears that had been building up all day spilled out of my eyes. My face scrunched up and my mouth trembled uncontrollably. He brushed his fingers through the wet trails, nuzzling me, dropping warm, light kisses on my cheeks. "Don't," he whispered. "Don't cry."

I didn't want to, but I couldn't seem to stop. I touched his waist when he drew back, my silent plea for him to continue even if I was falling apart in his arms. He answered with a deeper kiss, a skillful, attentive exploration that had my fingers tightening against the softness of his sweater. While he nibbled and teased and slipped his tongue between my teeth, he slid a hand back to cradle my nape, then he walked me backward, pressing me into the corner of my door.

His kiss transformed then, from soft and gentle to something else. I tensed, fearful of the sudden change in his demeanor. He stood like a wall in front of me, his muscular, sculpted physique pressed against my much smaller body. He didn't paw at me. If he was rough or clumsy, I could have pulled away and said, *ugh, this asshole*, and regained control of the situation, but he was the opposite of clumsy. Each touch of his lips, his tongue, ignited a response in me. His fingers twisted in my hair, his tugs causing pain but something pleasurable too.

His arm slid around my waist and tightened in a hard clasp, and in that moment something inside me awakened, some part of me that I'd stuffed down and smothered for years. That thing—want, desire— stirred to life with a starving vengeance. I returned his kisses with uncharacteristic abandon, and the harder I kissed him, the tighter his grip became. He had me cornered, but I found I liked being cornered by him. I wanted to be trapped and restrained against the wall and kissed into submission. I'd avoided passion and sex for years because I feared force, because I was afraid to give up control, but somehow he took all of that out of the equation and made me want him.

The more he kissed me the harder I cried, because it felt so good and so scary, and because each kiss was changing me a little inside. I grasped his arm with my free hand, clutching the rose stem in the other. I had to stop him before I lost myself, before bad memories and bad feelings turned this dream into a nightmare. I forced myself to stop responding, to push him away. His kiss gentled and his arm at my waist loosened. He drew back—only slightly—and pressed his forehead to mine.

"What is it?" His thumb caressed my cheek. "What's wrong?"

You brought me a rose. You kissed me. He wouldn't understand why that called for tears. He didn't understand anything. Instead I said, "I had a terrible day," which was mostly true.

He rubbed behind one of my ears, a light touch that made my breath shudder. "What was so terrible about it?"

"I don't know. I felt bad about last night."

"Bad in what way?"

I swallowed and turned my face from him. I shivered with cold, or anxiety, or perhaps the shock of his proximity. He drew away with a soft sound. "Where are your keys? Let's go inside and get you out of those wet clothes."

I understood from his words exactly what he wanted me to understand. *Let's go inside and fuck on some horizontal surface.* His gaze communicated it, along with the pitch of his voice and his gentle but possessive grasp on my arm. I understood—but old fears die hard. I wanted him but I didn't. I fumbled around in my bag, my fingers useless and heavy with nerves.

"I can't— I—" *I can't do this. I'm embarrassed. I'm afraid.* "I can't let you in. My apartment is a mess."

His hand stroked up and down my arm. He watched me with far too much attention. "Are you okay?"

I shrugged and flailed around in my bag for the keys. If I didn't come up with them soon I was going to fling the whole damn thing against the wall. "I'm fine."

He took it from me and within five seconds came up with the keys.

"Thank you," I said. "I'm sorry. I have to go change." I could really feel the cold now that he'd let go of me. I stared at the middle of his chest, wondering how to turn the closeness of this moment into a goodbye. The idea of it started my bottom lip trembling again. Why not me? Why couldn't I have this man and the things he offered? Why couldn't I be different?

"Ashleigh." He said it light and slow as I stared at his lips. "Let me come in, just until you feel better. We don't have to do anything."

I leaned back against the door, gripping the knob. "The thing is..."

"The thing is...?"

"I— I don't usually let anyone in my apartment."

"Why, what's in there?" he asked in a bemused voice. "Piles of dead bodies?"

No, I thought. *Just one dead body. My own.* I turned back to the door, opened the lock and edged myself inside. I intended to close it but something in the way he stood there stopped me.

"I don't want you to come in," I said. "I'm just... I'm just too weird."

He stepped forward, right into my apartment, and smiled at me. "Too normal, I'd worry about. Too weird is perfectly fine."

Waking Kiss and the sequel, **Fever Dream,** are now available at Amazon.com and other book retailers.

ABOUT THE AUTHOR

Annabel Joseph is a writer of erotic fetish novels that explore the drama, romance, and beauty of power exchange. She especially loves to craft stories that take place in the intriguing world of the Arts, and peoples her stories with painters, dancers, writers, actors, musicians and other creative types. Annabel makes her home in Atlanta, and loves to hear from her fans via her Twitter or Facebook page. Besides writing, Annabel enjoys walking, dancing, shopping at Anthropologie, art, playing Rock Band, and wearing vampy lipstick.

Find Annabel on the Web at www.annabeljoseph.com or follow her on Twitter at twitter.com/annabeljoseph.